"Julie, can't we finish what you started?"

With a breathy sigh her mouth fell to his. A moment it smoldered there, a ripple of flame racing between them. With dizzying abruptness he seized and dragged her to him. A low groan escaped him and his arms tightened about her with a violence that rocked her senses. She drew back, feeling faint, and heard distinctly, *"Julie, my God!"*

"Stop it, Ian!"

"Stop what? I know a woman's breathing. I know her sighing and the little sounds that escape her when she least knows it. And when her body is ripe and ready and surging to mine, I know that, too. You want me, Julie, just the way I want you!"

HEART OF THE GLEN

LILY
BRADFORD

A JOVE BOOK

HEART OF THE GLEN

First Jove edition published November 1981

First printing

"Second Chance at Love" and the butterfly emblem are trademarks belonging to Jove Publications, Inc.

Printed in the United States of America

Jove books are published by Jove Publications, Inc.,
200 Madison Avenue, New York, NY 10016

CHAPTER ONE

SLEEP, JULIE THOUGHT. If only she could sleep.

At this moment she'd have given a year of her allotted time on this earth to be able to switch off the wheels going round and round in her head. Or was it the wheels beneath her on the Glasgow to Inverness train—rickety-rack-rickety-rack-rickety-rack—keeping her owl-eyed and desperate for rest.

Rickety-rack-rickety-rack. She rubbed her eyes and stared for a scary moment into the mirror that her first-class compartment afforded. She shuddered. The healthy tan she remembered at the start of her journey had lost itself somewhere beneath a gray pallor that looked, she thought, terrific with the deep purple hollows beneath her eyes. Those eyes, normally blue and clear as a summer sky, seemed presently awash in their pink-stained whites. "I look...*awful*," she

1

gasped aloud. As if she'd been sleeping in the New York subways for a month! Only her hair, a riot of shining black curls that never submitted to control, still looked familiar, she thought.

A groan escaped and filled her compartment. But there was no one to hear. Thus far into the journey north she still had the compartment to herself and she was grateful. In these close quarters she could not count on herself to be civil to strangers.

Her head ached. Not a throbbing ache, merely a steady reminder that she could not recall the last time she had slept. *Really* slept, that is. Certainly not on the smooth British Airways flight to Prestwick, where the engines' steady hum, an apparent soporific to every other passenger aboard, had left her grappling with her wakefulness—and worse—through the brief night.

That "worse" was what really got to her. All those dark memories, dismissed so readily at home in the rush of business affairs, had roared in on her as if they'd been waiting to get her alone, and defenseless. What nonsense. All they'd managed to do was keep her awake.

Rickety-rack. She wished she were home. Wished she were back there in Southold on the North Fork where she belonged. She, Julie MacDonald Boland. She was crazy to let Shirley Wickam talk her into this trip...Rickety-rack...Shirley knew as much about the antique business as she did, perhaps more, Julie thought. She could have gone herself. "The trip'll do you good," Shirley had said. "Off with you," she said. And right now the only thing that could do Julie good was to go to sleep and wake up back home!

She was close to tears—but only from weariness, of course. She was not given to crying. She hadn't even cried when Gary walked out. So the feeling, now, of tears biting at her lids was purely from exhaustion.

Besides, all that other was long behind her, and she was not about to let her mind wander into that cave of hurtful things. She had promised herself, and she had surely kept that promise. She had lived from day to day, each morning at ten opening the shop for business, greeting her partner, Shirley, whose home lay just across the road, as if nothing had happened that was not meant to happen. So it was beyond her why Shirley should have imagined that she, Julie, needed anything to "do her good."

But then Shirl was middle-aged, long widowed, motherly and *romantic*, and could not be expected to understand that women today can carry on quite well, thank you, without a man on the scene. Shirley was still of that generation conditioned to lean on men, because nobody had ever told them that men, like cats, could be totally unreliable. Might as well lean on a blade of grass, Julie thought, turning her attention to the scene beyond her window.

There the Scottish Lowlands flowed by, sunless, damp, and mist-ridden, but green, greener than home, even now in late September. At another time, in another mood, she sensed the scene would be enchanting. Now it was all wrong.

It had been a silly decision on her part to go north at all. Everyone knew the center for antiques was London, or even Edinburgh. But no, some idiotic piece of sentimentality had prodded her at the last moment to choose the Scottish Highlands as a starting point. MacDonald country it was, and these many years later, Julie could still recall the dearest figure of her childhood—her grandmother—exacting a promise from her to see one day for herself the land of her birth, that she had left as a young "wifey." "My Heelands," she had called it. "My hame."

Nor did she fail to counsel her wide-eyed, nine-year-old granddaughter, "Go seek ye there a brawny lad. Och, grand men they are. Hard workers, hard drinkers, aye—but hard lovers, too."

Wherever old Ishbel MacDonald was now, Julie hoped she understood that *that*—that brawny-lad business—was the farthest thing from her mind. She was here solely to fulfill her pledge to Gran, and if in the process she could run across some extraordinary pieces worth shipping home for sale, that would tie it all up in one package. She was unlikely ever to come this way again, but once and for all, she would have touched down on the land her grandmother trod as a girl.

As the train slowed and drew into the station at Perth, Julie glanced through the window and winced. Oh, no. That much-too-jubilant crowd on the platform preparing to board the first-class carriage made her shrivel inside. If only they would avoid her compartment. But there were so many of them—a dozen and more. How could they help but spill over into her territory? As they filtered along the passageway, preceded by their laughter and gratingly cheery voices, Julie could only hope they were not traveling the three remaining hours to Inverness.

In a moment her compartment door swung open, admitting three tweedy ladies and two gentlemen. To think, she remembered ruefully, that except for Gran, she could have been luxuriating this very moment in a hot scented tub at a London hotel!

The compartment seemed suddenly to have shrunk to a tiny cubicle, choked with too much festivity. Julie, huddling in her corner seat, pretended sleep, and for a time the newcomers dropped their voices in deference to her. But it seemed impossible to drop the level of their gaiety, and gradually they were talking and laughing at a normal pitch.

Once, opening her eyes, Julie encountered one of the women watching her. "I'm sorry," the lady said. "I hope we haven't disturbed you?" Julie murmured that it was quite all right, and the woman launched into an explanation of the cause of their merriment.

It was a wedding they were all heading for, at Inverness, and it appeared that the young bride was their relative. Julie quickly gathered she was also their pride and joy, for the "bonnie" girl was marrying a "laird"—an heir to a huge estate.

Julie murmured polite acknowledgment and shut her eyes again without managing to shut out the chatter. It came to her hazily that the girl had "done right well by herself," reflecting glory on them all. In American terms she had grabbed herself a "catch," Julie mused, recalling no such family enthusiasm surrounding her own wedding to Gary

Boland five years before. Well, better luck to *you*, "bonnie" bride, she thought, settling back in her corner to the rickety-rack in her head and the slow countdown of the stations as the train climbed, laboring, into the Highlands.

She felt a touch on her arm and sat erect, staring at the apple-cheeked woman who had spoken to her earlier. "You've been asleep, miss, for half an hour. You're here. It's Inverness."

With an embarrassed smile, Julie thanked her. Smoothing her hair, she gazed a moment out of the window at the gray stretches of the cavernous station. One of the men traveling with their group had already brought her bags down from the rack and inquired now if she needed assistance. But no, she was quite all right, she told him. She had only to go as far as the Station Hotel adjoining the station itself, according to her travel agent. Anxious to be off, she bid her fellow passengers good-bye and followed the arriving crowds along the platform toward the exit.

Her brief rest had only whetted her need for sleep. She was by no means ready to take on the town. Her head was swimming and she wanted more than anything a hot tub and a bed to stretch out on, and a chance to throw off the jet lag that was dragging her spirits lower by the hour.

Emerging into the chill, sodden Inverness afternoon, she carried her bags across the few busy yards to the hotel entrance. She had not booked in advance; she had still been undecided about her destination when she'd purchased her flight. But the travel agent had assured her that autumn in the Highlands was definitely off-season. She would have no problem getting a room at the Station, or anyplace else she wished.

Her agent had not counted on a great Highland wedding, or the numbers of milling guests that confronted Julie when a porter relieved her of her bags and led her into the lobby.

It was a real downer. She waited patiently for the harried room clerk's attention, praying, with little else to count on, for a miracle. For just one small place, anyplace at all. A broom closet even. She ached for rest, and if God knew how she was feeling, he'd *make* a miracle.

But there was no room, and there appeared to be no miracle in the making. Certainly not in the person of the formidable lady who materialized at Julie's side as she begged and pleaded with the young clerk, "I'd be satisfied with anything, miss. I'm not the least bit fussy. If there's a bed—"

"I'm sorry, madam," the young woman said for the third time. "There really is nothing available. It's the wedding, you know."

The great high-domed lobby wheeled around her. In a moment, Julie thought, she would curl up on that stairway and—*die*.

A voice emerged from the din of the huge room, its tone matching the severity of the speaker's tailored tweeds. "What about the Caledonian, Valerie?" it demanded, bringing instant attentiveness from the clerk.

"*Ooh, aye, madam*, I telephoned there for a gentleman not half an hour ago. But they are full, too. There's the convention in town, and of course, *the wedding*—"

"The wed-ding, of course," the woman cut in with a curious sharpness on the word that made it sound as if she had bitten it off and expelled it. Without a pause she added, "Telephone Maggie MacPherson on Ardross Street, Valerie. She does bed and breakfast. She'll have a room. Tell her I said so. And now I shall take the key to my suite, please."

Julie scrambled frantically for words to express her gratitude, but the woman's imperious bearing overwhelmed her, as she had seen it overwhelm the room clerk. She managed only a meek, "Th-thank you very much," and knew it was not enough. The woman offered a bare nod of her head in acknowledgment and with a curiously intense glance her way, scooped up her key and left.

One glance, all the communication she allowed, and yet Julie had the distinct conviction that had anyone inquired, this lady could have told them everything there was to know about Julie Boland, American, down to the size of her shoes.

* * *

Mrs. MacPherson's bed and breakfast proved more than ample; clean, homey, and unstinting in services. Julie slept the night through and breakfasted heartily bright and early. It was impossible to resist the savory sausages and eggs that followed the Scottish porridge, and the kippers and scones that were warm and wicked with butter. She could not believe she had consumed the entire meal, but surely it, and the marvelously restful night, had lifted the pall under which she had arrived in Inverness. To think that only the day before she had considered leaving this evening.

She owed much, she knew, to the strange lady whose name Mrs. MacPherson dropped casually, as if Julie should know Mrs. Mairi Mackay quite well. Mrs. MacPherson had seemed to take it for granted that Julie was an acquaintance of the woman, and did not elaborate on her identity. Julie, unwilling to pry, hoped only that she might run into her again before she left for the south.

This day, a Saturday, Julie began a love affair with the city on the Ness River. For hours she rambled along its banks, crossing its bridges to and fro, roaming its old streets and older alleys, poking about its noisy marketplaces, and mingling with its people whose soft inflections brought her grandmother back so vividly in memory.

It was late in the afternoon before she reminded herself that she had business to attend to, and that Mrs. MacPherson had suggested some antique dealers nearby. With very little difficulty she found a thriving old shop on Church Street, its windows aglow with andirons, fire screens, pokers, and tongs. But for all their beauty, she quickly identified them as nineteenth-century items, and they were not what she was after. These things came to hand rather readily at home, she explained to the shopkeeper. She had hoped for pieces harking from Bonnie Prince Charlie's days. From the Forty-five. From Colloden. Items heavy with history.

Once in a while, she was assured, such pieces were uncovered in ancestral homes in the process of disposing of estates. But for the most part this shop dealt in such pieces as Julie saw about her—ornate clocks, silver condiment sets, salt dishes, a baby rattle.

Julie was considering a pair of silver tongs dating from 1780 when the shop assistant approached with the suggestion that she carry her quest to the nearby town of Beauly which he pointed out to her on a map.

"They might indeed have some interesting pieces since I understood them to have made a sizable purchase from an old estate rather recently." He traced the route she must drive to take her there, and Julie, making notes as he spoke, decided at once to hire a car for the following day. She had noted with a happy little thrill that Gran's village—Abriachan—lay between Inverness and her destination. Two birds with one stone, she thought, and thanked the man for his kindness.

She was about to leave when he tossed in another suggestion. "You might like to have a look in Grant's Close," he said. At Julie's blank expression, he explained, giving directions to another dealer, which she eventually located in a narrow alley off Baron Taylors Street, tucked away there as if shielding itself from a tourist invasion.

Julie peered through an ancient doorway and found a set of stairs rising above. There on the second story, in a series of tight little rooms, she gazed with delight at a captivating collection. But as her eyes roamed, suddenly it was one item that seized and held her transfixed.

It was hardly unique. It was of questionable value. Imitations abounded in souvenir stalls. Yet, as her fingers curled about the heavy glass paperweight in whose clear depths two lovers appeared to be running, her hand quivered, then trembled, shaking at last with such passion the tiny figures were instantly lost in their eternal snowstorm.

A moment longer she hesitated, hearing the shop assistant's "Can I help you, madam?" coming to her distantly.

Then astounding him, she let the paperweight rattle to its shelf, shook her head wordlessly, and fled.

She had barely reached the alley when the tears rushed to her eyes. For the first time. The tears she'd had no time for half a year ago. The tears she had so proudly withheld

because she would not be one of those women to cry for
a man. Even if that man was her husband, who walked out
one fine day, taking with him her love, her trust, her faith,
her heart, her whole life!

The glass weight had done it.

As she dabbed at her scalded eyes and groped her way
in the early northern dark through unfamiliar streets and
alleys, she was appalled that fate had had the gall to play
her such a shabby trick.

The last time her hand had curled around a glass paperweight—a twin, she could have sworn, of the one at
Grant's Close—she had sent it crashing against her gatepost
at home. She had not aimed it there, but it had missed its
moving target and exploded in glittering shards. Some must
surely lie there yet, she thought, remembering.

And her voice—how strange her voice had sounded to
her in the early morning stillness. So unlike her, raucous
as the crows swearing overhead, "Damn it, Gary Boland,
you can't do this to me!"

Looking back, hurling the thing had been futile, almost
uncalled for. He had not gone in anger. They had not been
screaming or raging at each other. He had left giving lavish
regrets and endless promises to return in a "few months,
a year. Give me a year, darling. I've *got* to do it. I'll be
back, you know that. I love you. I'm not *leaving* you. But
it's the first time I've been free. The first time I haven't got
my mother on my back. It's been so many years. *You* know
how it was—when you and everybody else were off at
college or traveling, I was here with her... never been
away... never been anyplace. It's now or never..."

He had been talking about it for weeks, ever since Margaret Boland was laid to rest. She had thought he was
daydreaming. Even when he began collecting things for his
trip, talking of packing this or that, she hadn't believed it.

Cold as stone she stood there listening, still not believing
he would go through with it until he walked out to his car
and slung his duffel bag into the trunk, and came to kiss

her good-bye. Too numb to act, she had felt his lips on hers but returned nothing. And he hadn't noticed! That was half the reason for her rage. She had given him lips of ice, and with his heart for the open road, he had gone without re-marking on her behavior. It was then that she hurled the paperweight, and missed his rolling car by inches.

CHAPTER TWO

IN THE MORNING, of course, she saw all that crying of the afternoon before for what it was, a delayed reaction to the wrenching upheaval in her life. As to love, of course it was real. What it was *not* was essential. Men were real, too, but entirely dispensable. She'd managed to get through half a year of her life without missing them. Not that she hated them all because one of their number behaved wretchedly. But only a fool would rely on one.

Okay. That was all behind her now, she thought as the little rented Mini cleared the bridge over the Caledonian Canal. Mrs. MacPherson's favorite "*ga*-rage" man, a Donnie MacLeod, had brought it around to the door while she was still at breakfast and cautioned her to remember to drive on the left. Julie assured him she would keep that in mind, but it being a Sunday in September, "Surely there won't be much traffic?"

"Except for the weddin' today, madam," he reminded her. "It's over at St. Ninian's, the one on the Cannich Road."

The wedding. She had totally forgotten.

"If you'll be travelin' along the lochside, you'll see quite a bit of it," he added.

"Abriachan," Julie told him. "I want to go there first. It's not far, is it, according to the map I looked at. I could get to Beauly after that, couldn't I?"

"Och, aye. Abriachan, is it? Then it's the Glen Urquhart Road you'll be wanting, the 82, and most of the weddin' guests will be travelin' that way, no doubt. So keep both eyes open, mum."

Julie's eyes were indeed open, but to the countryside, for it had turned into a dazzling day, the wet gray mists snatched and folded away by fingers of brilliant sunlight. Beyond the city, which fell back abruptly, she was caught up at once in the color of the countryside. The far distant mountains, already capped with snow, gazed down on yellowing fields and grassy stretches of unbelievable green. Stands of firs clothing the nearer slopes marched darkly to the lofty horizons. While below them, sleek fatted cows eyed the passing traffic benignly, and endless flocks of sheep grazed without pause.

Julie allowed the red Mini to dawdle along until she realized guiltily she was at the head of a long line of impatient drivers on a road too narrow and winding for passing. The wedding guests, she thought, reluctantly accelerating. Then, as if providing refuge, the Abriachan sign sprang into view and Julie darted for it, taking the road that climbed almost vertically, coiling and bumping its rutted way skyward.

Down below, she could hear the traffic she had just freed zooming along. But here, suddenly, it was silent.

And suddenly—it was Scotland.

Until now it had been for her an enchanting land, beautiful as the New York Adirondacks are beautiful. Yet until the Mini stalled at that point on the rise where the wild broom parted to reveal the deep cut that was Glen More, and terrifyingly far below, the somber waters of Loch Ness, it had not seized and shaken her as it did now. It had been Gran MacDonald's highly colored remembrances, an old woman's recollections heavily larded with sentiment. It had been a grandeur that never was, except in her mind.

Now as Julie's eyes spanned the remote reaches to far-off peaks thinly defined among the clouds, she knew the substance of the old woman's yearnings, and felt the first tug of this stark land upon her heart.

There was no rush about returning to the lochside and the scramble of wedding traffic. Ahead, here, at what seemed to her the top of the world, she urged the car along the single track that cut between miles of croft lands with their ubiquitous sheep, and cows, and rarely a stone cottage and a byre.

Yet it all must lead somewhere, and abruptly it led to a paved road that crossed and finished the narrow track on which she drove. Her choice now was a right turn, or a left, the road sign leaving much to her intuition since village names meant nothing to her, and her map maker must have thought so little of this junction that he omitted it entirely.

Pleasantly "lost," she chose the left turn, idling along for several miles toward a determined sun flashing in and out among scudding clouds. Wonderful day for a wedding, she mused. Lucky bride. Her own wedding day had recorded two inches of rain. And yet...

Rain or shine, who ever knows where the luck lies? she asked herself. One chooses a mate as blindly as one chooses a road where one has never passed before. Exactly as she had chosen a little way back. Cross your fingers, take your pick, and hope. How does anyone know where the chosen path will lead? Or, more tantalizingly, where the other might have gone?

Her full attention was drawn all at once to the road, philosophizing abandoned, for she had entered a stretch of sharp curves and perilously steep descent. She busied herself with her gears and thought of little else until with vast relief she arrived safely below. There, glancing at a sign pointing the way she had come, Julie groaned. What it said in effect was that if she had taken the *other* turn, all those miles behind her, she would have in due time reached Beauly where she wanted to go in the first place.

"Wrong again," she muttered, disgusted with herself. "Julie Boland, have you *ever* made a right choice in your life?" The truth was she had just executed a gigantic U and was once again on the very road, miles further along, that she had left escaping the wedding traffic.

Now it was either turn around and retrace her route up that awful, death-defying incline, with the little Mini probably stalling every few feet, or as her map now showed, explore this new road in its long, circuitous ramble to that same destination she had started for. Her instincts leaned to the latter. The wedding crowd would surely have passed this way and been lost somewhere by now. And so she turned to the right. Whereupon, her instincts being as bad as her luck, she chose the very route that led her several miles along directly into its lively midst.

"I can't believe it," she groaned, then put her mind to maneuvering cautiously among the lines of cars that had overflowed the postage-stamp-size car park of the picturesque stone church, narrowing the road to a squeeze. The church itself was so small, it was obvious many of those who had congregated in Inverness would have to content themselves with toasting the happy pair at the reception. But crawling along warily among the knots of fashionable guests—the women in their tartan silks and furs, their men magnificently kilted—Julie went breathless. The swirling reds and greens and blues and golds seemed to her more exciting on the men than among their bejeweled ladies. Their velvet jackets, gold buttons winking in the sun, accentuated the breadth of their shoulders and leanness of their waists above the graceful swing of woolen kilts. Their thick-knitted hose on sturdy, well-turned calves, gartered in reds and greens and blues, and their sealskin sporrans slung from their hips lent the final touch of elegance to the picture.

This is unreal, Julie thought, as if she had chanced upon a forgotten niche of the past that had somehow failed to catch up. This was her reward for choosing the "wrong" road.

Still this was *their* wedding scene, and she would have liked to be out of their way. She was just seeing an opening ahead when an attendant holding a white-gloved hand aloft blocked her path. She braked at once.

A chauffeured Rolls was approaching. As all eyes turned in that direction, Julie knew this was the bride herself arriving.

Delighted, she leaned forward in her ringside seat as the limousine crept to a standstill directly before her and the chauffeur hurried around to the passengers' door.

First to alight was a rusty-haired gentleman in a kilt of scarlet and green. Lace ruffles escaped the sleeve of his green velvet jacket, matching a spill of lace at his throat. But for all its splendor, it scarcely matched the pride aglow in his face.

He spun around at once, offering a hand to his daughter, and as she emerged in clouds of tulle, Julie could only gasp in admiration. The girl was a vision.

Slender as a young birch, there was still an appealing roundness to her figure, and nothing could conceal the prominent rise of her breasts—oddly at variance, Julie reflected, with the sweet, virginal face. As she stood brushing back a lock of her hair, the palest gold Julie had ever seen, innocence hovered above her like an aura.

Julie's throat tightened. However ideas might change, she thought, that girl is surely every man's fantasy of a bride—even, it would seem, with her obvious nervousness. Waiting for a starchy maid who stepped forward to straighten her gown and take charge of her train, the bride glanced about her, but Julie had a strong feeling she was not really seeing the guests lingering outside the church. She seemed in the grip of tension. Julie was sure she was not imagining it.

For the scantest instant, then, the girl's eyes, pale green and the shape of almonds, grazed Julie's, startling her.

She's scared stiff, Julie decided behind her wheel, but she had to smile. Small wonder. This obviously virginal bride had much to look ahead to—with fear, or pleasure, who could tell? With that face and that femaleness she exuded, and her bridegroom no doubt champing at the bit?

She'd be scared, too, Julie thought with a small shiver as the bride's party moved away and the white-gloved attendant signaled her on. She would be *deliciously* petrified!

Rolling again, the wedding excitement well behind her, she tried to recall being petrified on her own wedding night, but honestly could not. Gary had been, if anything, overly gentle, and very sweet, whispering again and again how much he loved and wanted and needed her (fighting words, they had become). But was there ever a word about her beautiful body driving him insane?

On a sudden impulse Julie pulled to the side of the road and stopped. Leaning to the rearview mirror, she stared with scathing candor at her reflection.

No, she squared with herself at length. Don't look for miracles. She was not that kind of a bride, and never could be. She was not even that kind of a woman.

Running slim fingers through that uncontrollable mop of curls, she examined her eyes, clear at last but—shrugging—a dime-a-dozen blue. Nothing mysterious, in spite of the thick black lashes fringing them. Nothing sultry, nothing alluring with nameless promises of delights. She narrowed them to gleaming slits, testing, then widened them quickly again. The only thing left was her skin, and thank the lord for small favors. It, at least, was clear, and free at last of the awful gray pallor of the journey. She had a nice tan left over from the summer—one teensy plus, she congratulated herself cynically. But nothing to drive a guy out of control. Her figure? Okay, she guessed, insofar as it was not bad. But she was never the bosomy kind she wished, and her height, at five feet three, consigned her forever to the Junior Petite racks in the dress shops.

She was not the sort of woman men could not live without, or even consider dying for. Or spent sleepless nights agonizing over. She awakened no raw passions in them, beastly or otherwise, and she lit not so much as a candle in their heaving breasts. She was in short a total washout as a woman, and it was a wonder that it had taken her so long to discover it. Why else, really, does a man walk away from his wife? Right?

That settled, she floored the accelerator. Okay, Julie, she said to herself, now go hunt your antiques!

Now her thoughts were centered on business. She would check out the Beauly dealers, and after that, on and down the A-9 back to Inverness, stopping only for a chance antique shop along the way. Tomorrow she would take the early train south to Edinburgh, later to London where the real treasures lay. There she might be fortunate enough to discover some fine chest or bureau, hopefully dating to the eighteenth century, no later, with drawers that could be filled with smaller pieces, silver, brass, and the like, to make shipping feasible.

Preoccupied, she lost track of the miles she drove, but later recalled that the road dipped steeply and that afterward she passed another ancient church and climbed again until, executing a string of blind curves, without warning, she nearly ploughed full steam ahead into the tail of an aging white Jaguar, and the idiot who had decided to change a flat at that ridiculous spot! The Mini screamed as Julie slammed on its brakes. Then she collapsed in her seat, breathing hard.

He looked up scowling beneath his bristling sandy brows.

"That was very close, madam," he muttered. His tone was edged with sarcasm, something she did not need at this moment in her life.

"It would have been closer still if I weren't such a good driver," she retorted with such emphasis her shining curls fell about her face quivering.

The scowl on his face leaped, then settled in again. His broad hand, in a gesture of exasperation, shoved back his thick hair that was sandy like his brows, but tinged with red. Julie, shaking from her scare, cared nothing for his exasperation.

"That's a dumb place to change a tire, mister, don't you think? Right at the bend in a narrow road like this?"

His jaw sagged. His look said he could not trust his ears. It also said something about women, but he did not translate it into words. He responded brusquely, "Would you care to suggest a good place to change a tire after a blowout on a road that's *all* bend, madam?"

She narrowed her eyes in defiance, but he was right, of course. That stretch of road lay like a snake that had writhed itself into rigor mortis. Nevertheless she waited for something other than that look of petty triumph to cross his face. A word of thanks was due her, she thought, for having deftly avoided an accident. But his scowl went darker, waiting for her to leave. He even started tapping a foot in exaggerated impatience, but her glance had dropped to the spare he was about to slip in place, and her eyes lit with amusement.

"How far do you think that'll take you?" Its threads were so worn, she thought she could see its lining.

His face darkened further, the muscles in his cheeks, hard as wire cable, springing into play. His eyes, twin slits of glistening anger, held her all at once, hypnotically.

She had never had this sort of a confrontation with a man. She had always been the first to give in, to step meekly back in her place. She had never seen a man *angry* with her before and visibly aching to grab and shake the daylights out of her.

Waiting for some outraged roar, her eyes grew large, her lips parted, and whatever lashing he had in mind emerged disappointingly frigid.

"*If* you'll be so good as to move along, lass, I might just find that out for myself."

She smiled. She'd had *her* little triumph. And as he stared back, she touched the accelerator and rolled a few yards ahead, only to brake again and look back through her open window.

"And what on earth's keeping you now, lass?" he called, exasperation returning. "I've a train to catch, will you be on now?"

It had passed through her mind in those fleeting moments that the man might really need help. Granted, he'd annoyed her; but she'd annoyed him now, too, and they were tit-for-tat even. If he needed help on this long lonely stretch, she just might suggest...

"What time's your train?"

"What difference?"

"The difference of getting there or not getting there!" she said crisply. "And if you'd like a ride, stop playing with that worthless tire and pile in."

Miles further along, Julie was still quietly laughing over the way he had jumped at her offer. It was almost pathetic, considering how she'd succeeded in raising his hackles, and how he must have hated to accept a favor from her. He was no doubt in a terrible bind, but he refused to talk about it even when she remarked sympathetically that she hoped whatever his problem, it wasn't too serious. He'd fallen silent almost at once, except for directing her, which wasn't much since at this point there was only one way to go. His tone had altered, however, going stiffly polite, though Julie sensed it was taking some effort.

He had an air, she decided after a fast appraisal, of having thrown himself together in a hurry. Beneath a well-worn Norfolk jacket, she saw a rough wool shirt, and surely those were riding breeches he wore. It was obvious he had reached for whatever clothes came first to hand in dressing for whatever mysterious emergency was driving him. Everything about him appeared hurried, even the way he kept leaning forward as if urging the car to greater speed with his body.

He had a pleasant enough face, she noticed, beneath that shag of sandy hair which he combed again and again with nervous fingers as often as he glanced at his watch.

"Relax," she laughed, "we'll get there." It was funny watching him press a phantom pedal each time she slowed a bit. It was also beginning to annoy her. He had finally admitted his train did not leave until five. "What *is* the rush?" she asked. "It's hardly three yet."

At first he did not answer. When he did, his scowl was back, blacker than ever. "I'm in a hurry, lass. If you'll forgive me."

But he did not meet her eyes, and it was not making

sense. Even she, a stranger on the road, knew they could not be all that far from Inverness. Then what was he drumming his fingers on the dashboard for, when he wasn't twisting the handle of the duffelbag at his feet? There was no way he was going to miss his five-o'clock train, she thought, easing into the A-9 where granted, the traffic was heavier, but moving along.

"You see?" he said. "And it'll get worse along the harbor."

She shrugged. "Then we could have done better to have turned around where I met you and gone back the way I came. That road was practically deserted—except for the wedding, that is. I'm sorry we didn't. Why did you want to go this way?" And after a rueful minute she added when he chose to remain mute, "I wish we had. I might have caught a glimpse of the bride again. And the groom. I'd love to have seen the groom."

There was no response. He was determined to be stiff and unfriendly and a real bore. Wrapped up in himself and his five-o'clock train. She was almost sorry she had bothered to help him. She could have gone on to Beauly and heaven knows what good deal she may have passed up.

Mr. Sphinx, meanwhile, was beginning to get on her nerves, his silence filling the car like tons of cotton wadding.

"Now don't tell me you hadn't heard about that wedding that everybody's been talking about. *I* heard about it before I ever got to Inverness." She was bedeviling him and was prepared to keep it up if he didn't answer.

"Aye. Heard of it," he mumbled at last.

"Oh? Did you know the families?"

"Might have," he answered grudgingly. "Many bearing the same names in these Highlands."

"But it's a very important wedding, I hear. Prominent people. There were even some guests on the train I came up on—the bride's family," she explained, "and I must say, they were terribly excited. It sounded to me as if the girl had made quite a catch."

"A catch, eh? You mean like . . . like a salmon? No little whitebait, I'm to assume."

Julie darted him a glance. If his face hadn't been stonier than ever, you'd have thought he was joking—except that he struck her as the kind of man who'd never made a joke in his life. Still he was talking at last.

"Not exactly that kind of catch," she explained, smiling. "That's an American expression, I guess. I'm—I'm American. This is my first trip here."

"Aye. Couldn't miss it."

"How?"

"Your speech, lass."

She laughed. "Of course. And I can just about understand you, too. But when we say a girl's made a catch, we mean—"

"That she's reeled herself in a big one. Aye, I know that very well. It's the same this side of the water."

"Oh." She felt let down. He had not laughed. He was so gallingly serious. But she resumed, because she had him finally talking, "Still a girl like that—she was gorgeous. I never saw a lovelier bride. I just hope her groom deserves her. So what if she did catch a salmon," she giggled again. "I'd say her salmon was doing very well for himself, too, and I think you'd agree if you knew her."

He was staring forward again, but Julie noted a subtle change. The hand that had drummed the dashboard was balled now into a fist, the skin drawn tautly over the knuckles, as if some inner tension was surfacing. Then, clearly, she caught a guttural sound from his throat as if he struggled to swallow a thing that would not go down. When it roared from him at last, she cowered and gripped the wheel hard.

"Her salmon's choking on her domn't hook, lass! You ken what I'm saying?" Rage touched his speech with pure Scots, and for the first time Julie felt his eyes on her. Burning. "If I know her, you ask? Aye, I know the lass well. And I'll not have her hook in my craw!"

CHAPTER THREE

JULIE FELT HERSELF shriveling in the heat of the anger of the man beside her. His outburst had staggered her, and she was not at all sure *what* she had in the seat beside her. His rage at the bride whom first he did not know, then decided he knew too well, seemed tainted with delusion.

"Can't you drive any faster?" he said, and she obliged without answering, wary now. Once he coughed lightly, and she remembered that "hook in his craw." A strange metaphor; though true, she had introduced the "catch" into their exchange, which had somehow triggered his fury. But why, she wondered? What was it about the bride's hook . . . and the salmon "choking on her domn't hook" as he put it? And always, "Can't you drive faster—faster?"

The light, little more than a candle's glow, seeped through the minutest crack in the basement of her mind.

She watched it move, painfully slow, but brightening, steadily brightening as it crept aloft. With a suddenness that sent a cry to her lips, shafts of light flooded every cranny of her brain.

"Oh, *no!*"

"Lass, what on earth are you slowing for? And now you've stopped!"

She pulled to the side of the road. A van went by, and a coal lorry followed. And others, two more before she answered, breathless at first, "I don't believe it. You—*you're* the bridegroom! Aren't you? Oh, yes, I can see it. You're the—Good heavens, what are you *doing* here? You're supposed to be at the church! *Your bride is waiting.* I saw her—that beautiful girl. *What's going on in your head?*"

"That is my affair, lass, and if you're taking me to the train, would you mind *doing* it? I've had enough for one day. For a lifetime, if you must know."

Julie's fury mounted like a rocket. It was no business of hers, and yet, envisioning that sweet young thing with a churchful of guests, waiting...not knowing...wondering...watching for him with those nervous green eyes...

"No," she said decisively. "I won't be a party to this underhanded sneakiness." She leaned back and crossed her arms for emphasis, unmoved even when his exasperation began rising to a wild pitch. In a moment she would order him out, but not before she'd spoken her full piece.

"I've heard of men doing rotten things to girls, but this—this is the worst." She clutched her arms closer, trembling a little with outrage. "Women are always on the losing end. Men do anything they damn well please. Listen bridegroom! I know what it's like to be deserted. It's awful, that's what it is. My husband walked out on me, too—"

"I salute him, lass, and may the wind be at his back!" He spat the words like grape seeds into the air, and she fumed at his insolence.

"Oh, sure, you would side with him. But what he did isn't half so low, so cowardly, so...so double-crossing, unspeakably *crummy* as what you're doing to that poor girl back there left to face a churchful of guests alone. Now if you expect to slink out of town on that train, you'd better start hitchhiking your way from here on, because it won't be me taking you there."

She expected him to bolt, licking his wounds. But he fell back on the seat with an audible sigh. There followed a weary groan, and then for a time silence, except for his fingers drumming again. She waited, and suddenly she understood.

"Oh, of *course* you wouldn't," she taunted him. "You're too well known around here. Everybody and his little brother knows you're supposed to be at that church getting married, fella! *Get-ting-married!* You wouldn't dare show your face. Am I right?"

He did not answer and she knew she was right. But he did not leave the car, either. She thought that in a moment she would insist that he do so, and returned her hands to the wheel hinting openly at her impatience. He seemed unaffected. But when he spoke again, his voice had altered. The sharpness was missing. "And what if I told you there are two sides to the story, lass?"

"Of *course,*" she agreed for the first time, and his eyes brightened. "There are always two sides." She drawled it, but he apparently missed her sarcasm.

"But I cannot tell you, I cannot speak of it," he added, softening his tone further. "It is not for a third party."

Her eyes came around to him then, wide, and for the moment even sympathetic.

"Naturally," she said, agreeably again, and he edged closer, confidently. "I do understand," she added, anger and contempt a thing of the past. "And honestly I don't want to know. That's between you and your bride. But why ever did you wait so long, until today, now, this very hour with the wedding in progress? Why didn't you thrash it out between you earlier? What you're doing, you *must* know is—despicable."

He sighed again. "Aye, aye, and I don't like it much, either."

"Then?"

"Perhaps, lass, there are even two sides to despicable—och, whatever, I cannot marry the girl. I can't. *I will not*. I must do what I started. I *must* leave."

"But I won't help you," she said evenly. "I could not live with myself if I did anything like that..."

Her words, breaking, trailed to silence. Her gaze had fallen to the wheel, and to her hand. And his, that had suddenly come to cover it. Enclosing it. His fingers curling ever so lightly around it. Her thoughts, her words, her intent, all riveted a moment, then scattered like marbles in disarray.

"And can I not persuade you?" she heard him say, but distantly, as though a singing in her ears. "Och, *can* I not, lass?"

He was pleading, his voice soft again, Scots again, and she was aware, and in a corner of her mind, wary. But her gaze was captive to the shape of his hand covering hers, and her senses alert to its warmth, its hard, firm texture, and to her own startling responses. She stared at it, incredulous, for too long a time, knowing that the merest effort would have brought her hand out from beneath his—*could* have easily, so lightly he held it. Yet there it lay as of its own free will, even when she felt her cheeks go aflame. Even then.

"You will, won't you, lass?"

Her eyes lifted to his face. She felt herself tremble, but only a little. Still he must have known. Yes, he surely knew. It showed in his look when she met it, and she read a kind of triumph there. Triumph brimming with relief. It was there in his smile, as well—the first smile he had bent on her— a broad one it was, with a catchy little quirking at the corners of his lips that for one, leaping, riotous instant tugged at her, deep, deep inside. And yes, she saw that he knew that, too.

Okay, win one, lose one, she acknowledged to herself.

But he'd made his fatal error. A fatal, stupid error, she thought. If he were as clever as he thought, he'd have masked it better. She would never have been allowed to guess he was playing her, using her. She herself was better at that game. He could not know what she was thinking. She veiled her reactions well, and her swiftly returning contempt for him. She even thanked him primly when he said, "Aye, you're a sweet lass after all, I knew you wouldn't let me down." Knowing what lay ahead, Julie almost felt sorry for him, seeing him relax and run his fingers through his thick sandy hair, relief flowing all over him. She smiled when he did and reached for the ignition.

Better for him if she had fumed at him, and shrieked at his arrogant male presumption that a smile, a few sweet words, were all he needed to charm females to heel.

"There's still time," he murmured, sure of himself now, as they started moving again, she hugging the side of the road, her eye sharp on her rearview mirror, sharper still on oncoming traffic. She waited for an approaching van and a lorry freighting lumber. He was watching her now, not the road. "I'll remember you, lass. I will."

"Oh, you will," she breathed. "I'm sure," and in that moment she spun the wheel, performing a perfect U-turn. Ramming the pedal, she was yards up the return road, the little car protesting, before he sat erect, shouting.

"Where are you going, lass? You're not heading the right way."

"Yes I am, luv," she retorted. "There's only one way and this is it. I can't get you to the church on time, but better late than never."

"Gir-rl, have you gone crazy?" he yelled, moving in on her.

"Not any more. Minutes ago, maybe," she confessed, "but not now."

The little Mini was not responding well to the speed she demanded, shimmying more than she liked, but she would not slow down lest he snatch the wheel from her hands and try some crazy stunt driving across her. He seemed desperate now, and raging mad. She persisted while he shouted, "Turn us around, gir-rl, and take me to the train as ye promised."

"I promised nothing," she lashed back. "*You* promised to attend your own wedding. And I won't help you break that girl's heart."

"What of my heart?" he shouted in her ear.

"You don't have one!"

"You can't do this to me. I won't be led like a sheep to slaughter—"

"Then jump. Go ahead. Any time you like. Jump—"

It was her last and final word, and it ended in a diabolic screech of brakes and rending metal as the Mini refused a turn and skidded toward its relentless rendezvous with a wall of stone that had stood for centuries.

Julie was picking fragments of glass from her clothing. Fragments of glass...

Her blazing fury had started draining even before the dust settled behind Gary's car. When there was nothing to be seen but the bare crest of the hill, she'd murmured, "Well, I guess that's that."

"What's that supposed to mean?" Shirley had asked guardedly.

Eyes to the ground, Julie moved down the walk and knelt beside the gatepost. Wordlessly she began collecting the larger of the glass splinters of the paperweight she'd hurled at the post. She was conscious that Shirley was waiting.

Without looking up, she spoke at length. "It means that now that his mother is dead, Gary needs a little hiatus from all his cares and responsibilities after those long years of anxiety concerning her support and health."

She was fully aware of the irony involved even before Shirley shot back, "*What* cares and responsibilities?"

She felt Shirley's eyes pinning her, but she resisted. After all, they had known some very good times together, she and Gary. They had been *in love*. It was impossible to dismiss all that as if it had never been. Woven into the fabric of her pain and disbelief was still a stubborn conviction that Gary loved her and would return, a lot sooner than he knew; and that the years of agonizing over Margaret Boland had taken their toll. Were it not for all that, this madness would never have overtaken him.

She looked up at last to find Shirley, arms crossed, plump legs firmly planted on the flagstones, clearly expecting an answer to her question. But as Julie started to explain, Shirley abruptly began expounding her own theme with deliberate disregard of any seeming intrusion on Julie's personal life.

"I've known you, Julie MacDonald," she began, and Julie flinched at the omission of her married name, "literally since before you were born. I was the first person after your daddy to know your mom was pregnant. It was I who drove her to the hospital the night you were born because you came early and your father was out of town at a dealers' convention. I helped bring you home and I was there all the time you were growing up. Now I claim the right to speak whether you like it or not."

She broke off, waiting a bare instant to see if Julie "liked it or not," but Julie remained silent. Everything Shirley said was true. Shirley was, and always had been a surrogate mother to her, especially after her parents' retirement and move to the West. She prepared to hear her out now, however painful it might be. And it was.

"You speak of Gary's responsibilities, and I must remind you that I knew his mother, grew up with her, and the fact that she's dead and gone doesn't change what she was when she was alive. She was a whiner and a crier. She died of emphysema but smoked like a chimney to the end. She leaned on Gary because he wanted to be leaned on. And he wanted to be leaned on because it was easier than having to go out in the world and make something of himself. Gary was totally without ambition; *you* should be aware of that, Julie. The situation was perfect for him. He could use it to toot around how he could never go to college because of looking after dear mama, who could, if he'd pushed it, have had someone in to live with her while he was gone. No, my dear. Gary didn't try for college because he was at the bottom of his high-school class. You know that, too, very well. Anyway, if he really wanted, he could have attended Suffolk Community nights and worked days as countless young people are doing all the time. And his mama could have hacked her life out over her cartons of cigarettes as she pleased. But all that aside, Gary could have become more than just the carpenter's helper he was when he worked his way into your heart—and bed, darling."

Julie bristled at this. "You *never* liked him, Shirley."

"The answer is no, since you bring it up. Nor did your parents."

That was true enough, but Julie had thought it was for all the wrong reasons. What was wrong with being a carpenter's helper?

Shirley read her mind like a double-page ad. "Not what you're thinking, my dear," she said. "There's nothing wrong with carpenter's helpers. But Gary would have remained one for the rest of his life, and never even aspired to become a carpenter, or anything else, if you hadn't brought him into your home and into the business when you married him. As a partner, no less." Here Shirley broke off sharply, and Julie flashed her a look beneath her brows.

"You didn't like that, Shirley, did you?"

"Of course not. As the senior partner in this business I resented it, but since your parents had signed over their share of the place to you when they retired, and you seemed determined to marry him, I loved you too much to put stumbling blocks in your way. I just hoped it might be the making of him, and I'll be honest enough to say he wasn't too bad at stripping and refinishing furniture, once you taught him all those fine points your daddy taught you.

"Oh, you did a lot for him, Julie—that he'd never have done for himself," Shirley continued. "But taking his mother into your house in her final two years, sitting up with her nights while he was sleeping, was far beyond the call of duty. Oh, don't think I don't know. I could hear her, summer nights, hacking away clear across the road, and I'd look over here at her lighted window, and sure enough *you* were there with her, not him! Used to make my blood boil. And so I ask you again, what cares and responsibilities does St. Gary the Martyr need that hiatus from?"

When there came no attempt at an answer, Shirley added, softly now, "Oh, my dear, I'm not trying to hurt you, but

a lot of us wondered whatever you saw in Gary Boland—
a girl like you..."

What had she seen in Gary Boland? At fifteen, then
sixteen and seventeen, there are things about a boy becoming
a man that can quite unexpectedly kindle a flame in a girl.
The first time she notices his face is no longer round and
pudgy, but lean, the bones beautifully sculptured. And that
he's shot up to six feet, and his legs on the basketball court
ripple with muscles. And that he's shy—so shy with girls
that when she spoke to him once after a game, he seemed
grateful for her notice. He had no girl. She was no belle
of the ball herself. She'd dated a little, but dances were a
worry. Sometimes she was asked, too often not. Now he
asked her every time. They were a pair. People spoke of
them together.

He told her he loved her at the last senior-class dance.
Spilled it breathlessly under a star-splattered sky with a
painted moon suspended over the Sound. She would never
forget, no matter what else followed. When he took her in
his arms and breathed, "I need you, Julie," to her his need
was his love and his love was his need. But that was a very
long time ago.

At college where she majored in art, his letters and phone
calls filled her with guilt if she dated anyone else. Holidays,
even weekends, she hitched rides from school ostensibly
to see her parents but in fact to help fill the void he felt
without her. He had steady work at a large new development
going up near Riverhead. But each evening he returned to
his mother's home, dutifully remembering her next day's
supply of cigarettes, the nails in the coffin that eventually
carried her away. And if he didn't have Julie to dream about,
he'd go crazy, he told her. He was so tied down...while
everybody else was living. He loved her. He needed her.
Comforting him, she always promised to come soon again,
and avoided her parents' unhappy eyes.

As their retirement approached, they had several rounds
about him, and she made an honest effort to break it off.
Relieved, her parents initiated the first steps of divesting

themselves of their share in the business, and the huge old
house adjoining the shop. The finalized documents were her
graduation gift, and she returned home afire with enthusiasm
for her new career—to the delight of Shirley Wickam.

The Gary thing she thought had been laid to rest. She
had not answered his last frenzied notes, and had avoided
his phone calls at the college dorm. Yet now that she was
home, it had to happen some time; and the day she glanced
up and found him filling the open door of the shed where
she was stripping an old teak chest, her world ground to
a stop. It was the old litany again; his love, his need.
His need. And he was powerfully handsome. And she was
ripe.

They were married two months later. Her parents did not
attend. Shirley did, having no out. Margaret Boland was
alone at last, except when Gary dropped in. Soon it was
Julie dropping in, without him. But she felt sorry for the
woman; so that eventually when she could no longer shift
for herself, it seemed natural to bring her into their home.

And yes, what Shirley had observed was all true. Gary
had left it all to her to cope with, while flooding her with
his gratitude. Were it not for the many sweet pleasures they
took in each other—it was perfect in bed, wasn't it? she
denying him nothing, however tired, he forever "grateful"—
Julie knew *now*, now that Gary was not there with his sweet
little smile, and all his "loving" and "needing" of her, that
she would have done well to have hurled that paperweight,
or anything else at hand, years before she did.

Two weeks later there came a letter. Gary was heading
South, he wrote. She was not to worry. He was happy. He
felt free for the first time in his life. He was doing what he
would have done years before if he hadn't been so tied
down. He would write now and then. He would wire if he
ran out of funds, but he was being frugal, stretching his
savings. It was why he did not phone, but elected to write.
He loved her; that was forever. If he stayed any length of
time in one place, he would send along an address so she
could write and tell him the news . . .

There was no news to tell him, Julie remarked to Shirley

after tossing Gary's letter her way to read. Except the divorce which her lawyer, Mike Patrick, had already set in motion, and that would not be consummated until the next spring.

Even Shirley was startled by the announcement. Julie had become closemouthed, and rigidly in control of herself and her emotions. Shirley scarcely recognized the pliant young thing she had known from infancy.

"You need a change," she told Julie one day.

"Do I? Why?" Julie sensed what the older woman had in mind. She smiled a crooked smile and without giving Shirley a chance to deny anything of the sort, she added, "If there's one element in this world I've had it up to here with, it's anything male, Shirl. I wouldn't even give room in my house to a tomcat."

Shirley let some time lapse before she began talking about a buying trip. Overseas. There must be some fabulous pieces to be found in Europe. France. Italy. England, even. "And, Julie, I just thought what a marvelous chance to visit your granny's home country."

"Shirley dear, you're as transparent as a piece of glass. And far more romantic than a woman of your age needs to be. Especially on my behalf," Julie laughed.

"Indeed!" Shirley countered with mock indignation. "But since you bring it up, girl, a little romance might just soften some of those sharp edges I see hardening around you lately."

"Soften—for whom, Shirl?" And with a touch of bitterness, "A lot of good soft edges ever did me. No, Shirley, I'm not about to go man hunting clear around the world."

These were the words of May. In September she did a total about-face. In sudden panic she grasped at the chance. Gary had phoned from Seattle. He missed her. He wanted to hear her voice. He was toying with the thought of returning. (Just toying, mind you.) The rambling trip had been wonderful, just what he needed. But maybe it was time . . .

"Did you miss me, honey? Julie? I can't hear you."

She hadn't spoken. Her thoughts were scattered, her feelings an enigma. For months she had imagined a moment like this; Gary phoning from somewhere to ask this very question, and she responding haughtily, "Oh, were you away?" Now it would not come. For the first time since he'd pointed his car up the road and over the brow of the hill, there was a need for searing honesty. This was the time to tell him to stay away—and her heart would not let her. It betrayed her. *A little of her still wanted a little of him.*

It stunned her, because she knew now what he was, and that surely she deserved better. Any woman did.

When she hung up, hedging, telling him nothing except that yes, she would mail him the check he asked for (his real reason for phoning?), she stood for a long moment staring into space. Staring across the sea, as it were.

After that it was only a matter of days—days pared close lest he return before she got away and her determination weaken; and she greet him with the slavish devotion that he seemed always to evoke in her.

"And what'll I tell Rover when he comes sniffing around for his bed and bone?" Shirley asked, driving her to the airport.

For answer Julie drew an envelope, stamped and addressed, from her handbag. "That's to mail from Kennedy," she said mysteriously. "The check he asked for, to 'tide him over.'"

"You're sending it? Oh, you foolish girl," Shirley gasped.

Julie uttered a short laugh. "Just something to help him celebrate the news that goes with it, Shirl. That by spring, travelin' man is going to be free as a bird. Or a stray mutt. In the meantime, if he has any questions, Mike Patrick our lawyer has all the answers."

She had voiced it without emotion, sitting up ramrod straight as Shirley maneuvered for a parking space in the Number 5 lot. She felt good about herself. Absolutely certain she had made the right moves. The only time her throat went tight was kissing Shirley good-bye in the British Airways terminal after her flight was called. There had been no tears for Gary, nor for the past, nor all the might-have-beens.

CHAPTER FOUR

JULIE'S FIRST RATIONAL thought of the present returned as she waited later outside the emergency room at the Raigmore Hospital. She did not even know how much later. There were still too many clouds of the past swirling and buffeting around in her head, but she was clear on one thing, one question that she addressed to Whomever was up there listening.

"Why God, why didn't it happen to me? Why did I get out of that accident without a scratch? Not one single bloody bruise? While he—"

She had been certain the man was dead. He was so white, crumpled with his head lolling to one side and his body angling unnaturally from a mass of bent and twisted steel. He looked ghastly. She had reached to touch him, then drew back in horror. She could hear her own screams rending the air, but could not stop, even when cars began pulling up and anxious faces leaned over her. Once it was the face of a police officer and he looked at her, not unkindly, striving to calm her. She sobbed, shaking her head from side to side, rejecting his comforting, wanting only to go back in time before it happened. Before she had taken it into her hands to direct his life . . . and then finished it.

There were questions, endless questions that she could not answer. He was dead. She knew it. They were trying to fool her, telling her he was breathing. He *looked* dead. Did they think she was blind? Crazy? The ambulance—it was no ambulance. It was a hearse to cart him away to the morgue. She was sure of it, no matter what they said. They were lying to her. They would not even let her touch him.

They were lifting him into the thing at last, and she pleaded hysterically to go with him. An attendant came and jabbed a needle into her arm, a tranquilizer that she hadn't asked for. But after that, she had grown calmer and her mind had cleared to a degree—enough that she grew crafty.

She had not wanted to be parted from him. She was distraught with guilt. She had to be with him if he returned to consciousness as they said he would. She wanted to be there at the very moment, to beg his forgiveness. She could not simply walk away from it.

She knew his name now. It hadn't surprised her when almost everyone who viewed him had reacted with shock. "It's Ian Fraser, the young laird!" she heard. "And bless us, he's being wed today." And "What was he doing so far from the church?" And "Ah, the poor lassie waitin' for him there."

It hadn't surprised her when all eyes swung to her for some answer. It was her craftiness that surprised her. That she could offer them such a garbled explanation that its very confusion was attributed to her state of mind, and put aside for later clarification. So in the course of it, she had emerged his "cousin from the States" who had met with him that morning and lingered too long on family matters, losing track of time . . . and he not yet dressing for the wedding, and . . . His car? He had had a flat, and they were using hers that she had hired the evening before (half a lie and better than none). But it was a time when the truth would not do, less for her sake than for his, for she had done him damage enough as it was.

Then, just as she recoiled from her own bald glibness, in one shining moment Julie lied again, lifting forever the blame of desertion from Ian Fraser's shoulders—or so she hoped.

"Oh, don't you see? It wouldn't have happened if we hadn't been speeding so fast to get him to the church!"

And so the victim's "cousin" had sat with Ian Fraser in the ambulance, the sirens blaring overhead on the long ride to Raigmore. Her eyes never left his face, into which she thought some color was returning. "He's looking a little better, isn't he?" she queried the attendant hopefully. "Oh, aye," the young man answered. "A mild concussion, likely. There's a fracture of the leg, however. And possibly internal injury that we'll soon find out." And then, "Och, it's a shame about the poor lass at the church. I wouldna want to be the one to tell her. And all the guests still waitin'."

Outside the emergency room Julie wondered how long it would take to bring the girl to his side. She wanted so badly to see Ian Fraser before anyone else arrived, because later would be too late. She would suddenly cease to be his "cousin" and cold eyes would direct her to leave.

The wait seemed interminable. Without warning, then, the doors were flung open and two nurses began wheeling a sheeted figure on a stretcher toward a long corridor.

Julie sprang to her feet and followed, but they signaled her back. Yes, it was he, but no, she could not speak to him yet. She glimpsed his face. His eyes were shut. She could not tell if he was conscious. "He's going to be all right?" she whispered, pleading.

"Ooh, aye, he's coming around," the young nurse nodded. "You may see him after a while. When we settle him in his bed."

After a while stretched to eternity, Julie thought, agonizing over her chances of seeing him at all. She wondered that it was taking Ian's fiancée so long to arrive, and crossed her fingers that it might take longer. The nurses had forgotten her, she was sure of it. Nearly half an hour had passed. Then, abruptly, one of them stood before her.

"You can go to him now," she said. "He's awake at last, though a wee bit groggy. I'll take you there."

Julie followed along from ward to ward, and finally to one where every bed was occupied by men in casts, or in traction, arms and legs protruding grotesquely at every angle. She dreaded trying to talk to him with so many others about. Then she saw to her relief that the nurse stopped beside a curtained area forming a private cubicle.

The nurse rolled back the curtained "door" and ushered her through, reminding her not to remain too long. Julie's heart pounded, hoping for a few brief minutes alone. She heard the nurse's cheery greeting, "Now how are we doing, Mr. Fraser? Good? Fine. There's a pretty young lady to see you. I've given her only a few minutes."

Julie waited, taking a tentative step toward the bed. She caught a mere glimpse of his face beyond the bulge of a light blanket. His eyes were shut, but the knit of his brow, familiar now, was very much in evidence. She wondered if he were in pain, and quailed before a fresh onslaught of guilt.

When he spoke, his voice seemed thick, doubtless from his medication, and slow, each word hauling behind it another word until the statement was whole, and wholly unmistakable.

"Tell her—go way—don't want—see her ever—ever—again."

The nurse cast a look of dismay at Julie. "Och, now that's bad—"

"No, please," Julie whispered. "I won't stay. I promise. But I must talk to him." And before the nurse could block it, she took a swift step to his bedside and leaning to him, told him softly, "Ian—Ian Fraser. Please, please listen to me. Even if you hate me forever. Listen, and then I'll leave and not bother you again."

She waited in the straining silence for some altering of

his wooden expression. Slowly his eyes slitted, and fluttered open, focusing on Julie's face.

"Och, *you*—is it?" he murmured, still with effort, but she could detect no trace of the hostility he owed her. The nurse, with a half smile of uncertainty, left them alone. And there followed a thing so bewildering, Julie's apology faltered before it ever reached her lips.

He grinned.

It was a weak, lopsided grin, and it might have been a grimace of pain, she thought. But his voice reflected no such discomfort. He said, "Hello," a shade more firmly now. "I thought for a minute it was that other one."

She saw his error and hastened to help clear it up. "I'm afraid it is, Ian. You're still a little dopey, aren't you? It's the drugs they gave you, I'm sure. You're not seeing clearly—"

"Clear enough, lass."

"I'm the *American*, Ian, remember? The one who—"

"Aye, know you well, lass," he said. The medication was wearing off and she was relieved, hearing his voice strengthen. Yet she was skeptical.

"Why aren't you raging mad at me?" she asked gently. "I did a terrible thing. I don't know how to make it up to you."

The grin was back, and her own lips curved into a trembling smile. "I'll think of a way," he said, and laughed, and winced and screwed up his face in pain. "Don't make me do that, lass. It's the rib that's cracked."

"Oh, I'm so sorry, Ian," she cried, leaning to him. "I cannot tell you how sorry I am. I wish I could help. I've caused you so much trouble." She sank into a chair at his bedside and without thinking, laid a soothing hand on his.

"That's a fair start," he said. "But och, you saved me trouble, too, lass. I'm still not wed to Audrey Grant and there was no need to leave the land to stay that way. I didn't want to be going at harvest time. Need every hand now."

It crossed her mind she knew so little about him, and yet she was sitting with him so—almost intimately, her hand that she had laid carelessly on his suddenly *in* his—and all of his doing as he spoke. She did not withdraw it. She did not think he was aware what he had done. It was a reflex action, no more. He was thinking aloud, the things he spoke of rather meaningless to her.

"There'll be the sheep, too, to transport to the lower pastures. Aye, it's a busy time—"

"Ian," she broke in quietly, and then searched for words. "You're not really going to be doing any of those things for quite some time, you know. A fractured leg, a cracked rib, and heaven knows what else."

"Aye, I know that, all right. But I have good men. They need only a word from me, directing them with what's to be done . . ."

His words trailed. Died. She saw for the first time how close their heads had drawn, and that he was gazing into her eyes, and that she could not draw her own away—and did not want to. A vagrant thought, utterly independent of logic, kept threading blatantly among the serious points she had been trying to impress on him: he is terribly good looking, hadn't she noticed? But of course she did, right from the start. She was simply not about to admit that, she was in no mood for that, but it's all right now . . .

She pulled herself erect in the chair.

"What's your name, lass?" he asked abruptly.

"Julie," she said.

He studied her until a warmth flooded her cheeks, and her lashes dropped their sooty black upon them.

"That is all?"

"Boland," she answered after a moment.

"Miss? Mrs? Or that confounded Ms?"

She smiled. "Mrs."

"Oh? Och yes, you told me, he deserted you. Aye."

She laughed aloud for the first time. "You congratulated him."

"Aye, I did that, I remember now." He went thoughtful a moment. "That is what you spared me, Julie Boland. Spared me leaving her later. And I would have. Immediately after. Or some time. Better before the wedding than after, with maybe a child or two if it lasted that long."

She stared at him, shaking her head. "You cannot mean this. It's *cold*-blooded, Ian. You asked this girl to marry you."

"Aye, I loved her."

"When did you stop loving her?"

"This morning."

"This—*morning*? You *couldn't* have, not so abruptly. But oh, *I* know what was wrong with you." She leaned back, chin in hand, surveying him like some odd specimen. "You just got cold feet, that's what happened to you. You realized all at once you'd be parting with your precious singleness."

"Lass! I was liking you—"

"It makes no difference what you feel for *me*, Ian. I'm not the girl you left in such a humiliating position at the church with all those guests who'd traveled so far."

"I am tired of the subject, lass."

"But you're going to be hearing a lot of it, Ian, from everybody, your friends, your relatives, and hers, too, I'm sure, if you don't rethink what you're doing. And the chance is wide open, Ian. Only you and I know you were trying to duck out. I've covered for you—"

He groaned. "You needn't have bothered. I won't be thanking you for that. They'll all know soon enough there'll not be any wedding."

"But you can't jilt a girl at the altar, Ian, and expect—"

"Julie—"

"But it's unfair, and forgive me, it's downright dishonorable."

A growl rumbling from his throat stopped her. "Are you lecturing me again, lass? Is there no end to your interfering—even after...after this?"

She hesitated, bending to him again. Beyond the curtained cubicle, voices were drawing near, the nurse's which she recognized, and another—unquestionably the young bride herself—frightened and bewildered. Julie seized this one last moment, intending to plead with him for common sense, and for his own good reputation. She bent lower, the

words on the edge of her tongue: think, please think, don't
destroy her, do the right thing, you'll never regret it. Then
she hung a moment too long above him, the words frozen
in her mind, fathoming his eyes, remarking to herself that
the sandy shade of his hair did not extend to his lashes that
were thicker than a man's needed to be, and a very rich
brown; a pleasing contrast to those eyes themselves which
were clear and warm and gray—when he was not angry,
as now, but forthrightly returning her gaze.

The sounds beyond the cubicle were closer. She would
say what she intended in haste, and run. Her lips parted.

And then she bent and kissed him. Full on the mouth,
and clinging a breath overlong.

Her face burned when she withdrew, coming lithely to
her feet. She could not look at him. She was appalled. He
had not responded. Even his hasty, "You're a strange one,
lass," sounded chilly. Or was shocked the word?

She must have been crazy. Why had she *done* it? She
longed to escape unseen. But the curtain rolled back on its
bar, and the girl stood there, the nurse in the fore blocking
Julie's view, as well as her exit.

The girl—Audrey he had called her—had taken time to
change from her wedding gown to a slim suit of beige suede
topped with a narrow mink collar. She'd lost none of her
breathtaking beauty in doing it. There were no tears, or hint
of them in her eyes. If anything, Julie thought she looked
numb.

She yearned to be gone, having no wish to witness their
emotions toward each other, if ever they broke loose. The
girl seemed unaware of her, and edging behind the bulky
nurse, Julie waited for her chance to slip away. She was
nearly at the curtain when she caught their first exchange;
the girl's low, and controlled.

"Really, Ian. I don't know whether to forgive you."

And his response, "Don't trouble yourself, Audrey, I'm
in pain enough already." It was brutal with sarcasm, Julie
thought. And even if there'd been a recent lovers' quarrel,
as was obvious from his attempted flight, it was a cruel,
cruel thing to say. But all that aside, why hadn't she rushed

to his side and thrown her arms around him? Didn't she realize she had almost lost him? Or had she been shocked by events into a kind of stupor?

Searching for the hospital exit, Julie felt dazed. Even she, who barely knew the man, had ached so terribly to comfort him. To—to kiss him. She hurried on, feeling a sudden throb at her temples. Her little moment of truth was not precisely easy to face. Oh yes, she had ached to comfort him, but that was not it. Not all of it, she thought, taking herself to task.

She knew what she ached for. *She wanted to kiss him*. And *that* was it, that was all of it. She liked that mouth of his the first time she looked at him. Even when he was using it to bark at her, she wanted to run her fingers along his lips, and know what they'd feel like on her own. It was the real reason she kissed him. And she still didn't know what they felt like, because he did not kiss her back. She could never forget that. He had looked at her, called her strange, and let it go at that.

Oh, but it was absurd. She was making too much of it. She was glad all at once that it was over. She had gone to him. Apologized. Done her bit. And carried on like a fool!

And no, it was not over. Like it or not, something of it had lodged in her head, or her blood, or somewhere. She did not like the term "heart." It was too serious. But it wasn't going to matter anyway. She was going to pull the plug and let it all drain out.

Simple enough, because she would never be seeing him again, and that was as well. Gary had not made a man-hater out of her, but she was not about to put her heart on the line again. No way. She might have a relationship now and then, but it would not involve her heart.

She found the door at last to the parking lot, and stepped through, staring blankly before her.

What was she doing in a parking lot? She had no car. Another worry. She would have to make amends for that. Mrs. MacPherson who'd gone to the trouble of finding one for hire would be upset, to say the least. But for the present, how was she to get back to Mrs. MacPherson's?

She glanced up at a soft gray sky just beginning to spit rain. She felt alone, and suddenly wracked with loneliness. It was not her way. She had not known loneliness in her past. She had been self-sufficient, involved in all things around her. Yet now, and here, in this foreign place, loneliness sought her out and came rolling toward her, a great dark tide threatening to drag her under. She stifled a need to cry, and coped with it well, leaning on the wall at her back. She was frightfully tired, of a weariness that followed emotional trauma rather than activity, and she had had her share of both.

She glanced about and decided to walk to the road that bordered the hospital and look for a cab. Or try to catch a ride into town, or something. She waited for a car to pass, and then as she stepped from the walk, another, black and shining, pulled up directly where she stood and stopped.

She moved to one side as a chauffeur emerged and opened his passenger's door, assisting an elderly woman to the narrow pavement. Suddenly Julie and the woman stood staring at each other. Mrs. Mairi Mackay was the first to recover.

"Well, young lady, and how are your accommodations at Mrs. MacPherson's?"

"Oh, I'm so happy to see you again. And so grateful. Everything was just fine."

"I'm glad to hear that," Mrs. Mackay said with a quick nod. "Strange meeting you here."

"Oh, yes. There's somebody I know who was just taken in. An accident."

"Really!" She shook her head. "So many of them lately. People drive like maniacs."

Julie reddened. "I'm afraid I was driving. And yes, you might say that."

The woman's brows leaped. "Indeed? Well, I'm glad to see you escaped injury. If you'll excuse me, I have a patient to visit, too."

Julie nodded, and stepped aside. Mrs. Mackay started for the door, then swung around all at once. "Did you say you were driving? Where's your car?"

She laughed nervously. "In car heaven, I'm afraid."

"*Really*. Then you'll need a ride, won't you?" Without waiting upon her answer, she addressed her chauffeur. "Richard, do please take the young lady to Mrs. MacPherson's and then return for me."

She was her guardian angel. Julie sighed, sunk deep in the leather luxury of the BMW, proceeding noiselessly toward the Eastgate and the town. Every time Julie needed help most, she appeared. She hardly deserved it.

She supposed she didn't deserve, either, Mrs. MacPherson's motherly concern for her when she returned. "The police had the wreckage towed to Donnie's ga-rage, but it was you we worried about, having no word. I'm surely relieved to see you, Mrs. Boland."

Donnie had left word not to worry, he was insured for such things. But when she had washed and freshened up, Julie walked around to his garage carrying a bottle of Scotland's finest.

"Oooh, now, it waren't necessary," he beamed. As she paid for the day's rental, he asked, "Now will you have a wee dram, miss? Ye must be needin' one sure."

Julie declined the dram as well as his offer to rent her another vehicle. She would be leaving next day, she told him, forbearing to add that absolutely nothing had gone right for her in this north country. Either it, or she, seemed jinxed.

At the moment she wanted only to get back to her room and clear her head with a good night's sleep. She thought of passing up Mrs. MacPherson's evening meal just to be alone with no need to talk. But Mrs. MacPherson was waiting for her, with a message and an undercurrent of excitement in her voice and in her round pink-cheeked face.

She read it aloud to Julie, exactly as she had taken it down over the phone: "Dinner at the Station Hotel with Mrs. Mairi Mackay. Eight thirty, and please be prompt."

Julie's eyes widened. "Oh. How sweet of her," she said

in a small voice. "Though, oh, I'm so tired, and I'll be leaving in the morning. Do you think she'd mind if I sent regrets?"

The look on Mrs. MacPherson's face stopped her. "I'd be sure to go this evening, Mrs. Boland, if I were you. She is a very important lady."

She endowed the last, Julie thought, with the awe generally reserved for a royal command appearance.

"Besides," she added, whispering suddenly, "it is with *Mrs. Mackay's grandson* you were drivin' when your car smashed into the wall."

CHAPTER FIVE

PRECISELY AT HALF past eight Mairi Mackay descended the grand staircase of the old hotel, and Julie rose from the chair in the lobby where for the past quarter hour she had sat and quaked. The link of events still challenged belief, but as Mrs. MacPherson had pointed out, smiling at her open-mouthed astonishment, "We're very close up here in the Highlands. We know each other well, and many of us are related. Myself, I was kitchen maid for Frasers, a cousin of Ian's father, before I married Gordon MacPherson. He's dead now, but when he was a lad, he went to school with Ian's mum for a time before she went off to a young ladies' academy in Edinburgh. Now of course, she was a Mackay and it was Alasdair Fraser she married right after the war and *his* mum was a MacKinnon, and . . ."

Julie's head reeled, but Mrs. MacPherson had at least

instilled in her some comprehension of the tightness of these Highland families. She felt like a stranger, an outsider, and never more so than in this moment, watching Mairi Mackay approaching, nodding to personnel who paused each time to bow as she swept by them.

Mrs. Mackay was wearing a formal dinner gown of a gray crepe de chine that fell in graceful folds from shoulder to floor. Julie, cowed by it, thought she resembled a flagship steaming out to sea; the bowing bellhops little tugs saluting. She wished she had had the good sense to select something more appropriate from her limited wardrobe than this slim dark silk suit that she had grabbed in her confusion; though anything she wore would have looked shoddy alongside this woman's overpowering stateliness.

There came that exact moment when Mrs. Mackay acknowledged her presence, though Julie was certain the woman had been aware of her from the broad upper landing. She cringed. The lady was going to make this very difficult, she could tell. It crossed her mind that she didn't know quite how to handle the matter; especially the matter of Ian's attempt to dodge his own wedding. She had a conviction that Mrs. Mackay would not have approved. That is, if she knew! It came to her abruptly that she had no way of telling what Mrs. Mackay knew. How much, in fact, she was meant to know. And if she, Julie, ought to be the one to tell her. She had a fear the woman would worm it out of her, if she had any suspicions at all. She hoped she could avoid discussing it; though how anyone avoided discussing anything with this imposing woman was beyond her. All she was certain of now was that Mairi Mackay had not asked her here—no, *ordered* her here—solely to have company at dinner.

As Mrs. Mackay touched the lowest step, Julie advanced to meet her.

"Good evening," she said, loathing the tremor in her voice. "It was good of you to ask me."

"Ah, yes," came the answer, and after a subtle pause, "Mrs. Boland. Nice of you to come on such short notice."

Julie knew this was no more than a polite pleasantry and

that Mrs. Mackay would never have entertained the possibility that she might not come. For an uncomfortable moment Julie felt her face being studied intently, and a slow flush spread to her hairline. She wished her hostess would get on with it.

As if she read her guest's mind, Mrs. Mackay turned and led the way into the main dining salon, where the lavishness of its softly lighted elegance lent emphasis to Julie's sense of inadequacy. She wondered if Mrs. Mackay was not perhaps having second thoughts about inviting her.

The headwaiter, seeing her, stopped what he was doing and hastened to escort them to a table. But Julie noticed Mrs. Mackay needed no escort. She swept him along in her wake, steering for a table in a far corner with a reserved sign prominently placed. Julie had the feeling no one, ever, occupied this table other than Mairi Mackay.

She never after recalled what it was she was served, though her hostess had recommended one magnificent dish after another, and Julie taking her cue accepted all. What she did remember—was never to forget—was Mairi Mackay's straight-on-target opening gun.

"Well now, Mrs. Boland, you've certainly left your mark, haven't you?"

Julie grew warm clear to her toes. But Mrs. Mackay was not finished. "Tell me, my dear, what are you after in this part of the world? That is, what *really* do you have in mind?"

Julie's eyes lifted cautiously to the face across the table. Square of jaw and broad of cheek, with traces of reddish hair still holding fast amidst the gray of her short, no-nonsense hairstyle, it was the face of countless other elderly Inverness ladies she had encountered since her arrival.

Only the eyes were different. They were black. Unqualifiedly black. And they snapped. And sparkled. And danced. And penetrated very deeply into her own, unsettling her wildly, especially accompanying that question she had cast like a trout line before her guest. "Bite, little fishy, do bite," they teased.

What does she know, Julie wondered uneasily, and what does she *want* to know? What did Ian tell her, for heaven's

sake? Surely not about that stupid kiss, which of course
would have been an ego trip for him. But would he confide
such a thing to his *grandmother?* What did she *mean* asking
what she had in mind?

It angered her a little, but Julie was in no position to
respond haughtily. The woman had been too kind to her.
Besides, Julie had a distinct feeling that no matter what she
answered, it was of small importance—that Mrs. Mackay
was speaking from a prepared script, and the farce would
come to its logical conclusion when she was ready to con-
clude it.

She evaded the point of the question neatly enough, she
thought. "Certainly I did not have in mind wreaking such
havoc, Mrs. Mackay. And I must tell you that after everything you did for me, I am absolutely mortified, about your
grandson—"

The black eyes turned a shade blacker, and the strong
mouth thinned, but for a mere second. Then with a careless
shrug, Mairi Mackay said, "Oh, that. Yes. Of course. But
it was not fatal." She paused, thoughtfully, then tossed her
head. "He'll certainly have plenty of time to think things
through now."

Julie was mystified. There had been no clear reference
to Ian's intentions to jilt his bride. And what was he supposed to be thinking through? The pros? Or the cons? Julie
felt her way warily. "I only wish I had nothing to do with
it, Mrs. Mackay, I feel I contributed to the whole disaster—" She paused, detecting a flicker of a smile, there and
gone, at the corners of Mairi Mackay's lips that struck her
so like Ian's she had to catch her breath and begin again.
"I mean, I realize it was not my place to—to—" she faltered.

"No, I suppose not," Mrs. Mackay returned promptly.
"It *was* rather aggressive of you." She did not meet Julie's
eyes saying it, and Julie sensed that in spite of a mild
displeasure in her tone, something was not ringing true.

She's not saying what she's meaning, Julie realized.
She's skirting something. This isn't what she brought me
here for.

"Do you like those prawns, Mrs. Boland?"

"Those—oh yes, they're delicious, Mrs. Mackay."

"I think you will enjoy the Bisque de Homard Cognac, too. They do it so well here."

Small talk, Julie thought. Prattle. But through it all there leaked an air of something waiting, waiting to be exposed. She took the lead for once.

"How did you find Ian—uh, your grandson, Mrs. Mackay?"

"Complaining as usual. Of course, Audrey was there when I arrived—his fiancée. She left soon after. Rather quickly, poor girl." Julie thought it odd she should mention that. "And he ranted all the time I was there. He was in a foul mood. Though I'm sure he's not very comfortable, but with even a simple fracture, he can't hope to be on his feet for a while and he'll simply have to accept that. He has good men at his croft. They can handle what needs to be done—the barley and oat crops and all that. Still," she reflected, "there was no reason to carry on the way he did. He was fortunate to be alive. And so were you, Mrs. Boland."

"Yes, I know that," Julie murmured. Then, submitting to a devilish urge, she added, "I hope they've managed to set a new date for their wedding."

Mairi Mackay's black eyes flashed her a look. "Oh, do you really?"

"Y-yes," she answered, uncertain all at once. "Anyway, I'm sorry you found him so—"

"Nasty?"

Julie smiled, not knowing if Mrs. Mackay meant to be funny. "I hope," she said, "it wasn't anything I'd said. Or done?"

"Why?" Mairi said, frowning at her last remaining prawn. "Had you done something?"

Julie bit her lip but her hostess appeared not to notice. The waiter removed their crystal bowls and returned with the bisque before she resumed. "You haven't told me, my dear, what is it you hope to find in these Highlands?"

"Antiques," Julie answered at once. The only way to get

around all that deviousness, she thought, was to confound her with flat out answers. And oh yes, she was a devious one. The worst kind; the kind who manage to sound so straightforward while turning and twisting their questions and your answers until they've learned whatever they're after. Then why did she go on liking her, she wondered? It defied all sense, but the truth was Julie liked, even enjoyed, this Mairi Mackay.

"Antiques, is it?" she said now. "I thought so. Maggie MacPherson mentioned it and I couldn't let you get away without seeing some of the pieces I have at Glenshiel House. That, my dear, was why I asked you for dinner this evening."

That is not why, Julie thought. That is an excellent excuse, but it was not why. Still it was a pleasant enough game, and she didn't mind playing it, and for all she knew, the woman might actually have something interesting.

Glenshiel House, Mrs. Mackay explained, was her home, the hotel suite she maintained as a convenience for events in town. "But I'm going back tomorrow. You may come by to see me there. In fact, you might as well plan on staying a few days."

Julie was not certain. The woman came on strong. She was a presence. To be in her company too long could be stifling. The very way she presented her invitation—*telling* Julie, not asking her—put her off a little.

"I don't know, really, Mrs. Mackay. Actually, I was off for Edinburgh on the eight-o'clock train."

"Really!" she answered, her tone implying that Julie must surely know that could be of no great importance. "Ah yes, too bad. I do really have some unusual pieces to show you that I'd be just as pleased to dispose of."

"Such as—?" Julie could not resist.

Mairi Mackay's eyes grazed hers and looked away carelessly. "Such as, among other things, a seven-hundred-year-old table, my dear."

Julie gasped. "I'll come." And again, to be sure she had been heard. *"I'll be there, Mrs. Mackay."*

Mairi Mackay smiled. "I shall send my car. Shall we say Wednesday? Maggie MacPherson will hold your room for you. If you want it again. I've already told her."

Was any seven-hundred-year-old table worth it, Julie wondered, pummeling her pillow at three twenty-nine in the morning. It was the second time sleep had abandoned her on this wretched night, and her own idiocy in bending to Mrs. Mackay's invitation for the sake of a piece of furniture was tearing at her now.

Earlier, when she had crawled, bone-weary and mentally drained, between Mrs. MacPherson's flannel sheets, she was sure she would drift off to sleep like a babe, and in the morning everything would be just fine. Now she rose up in the icy room, drawing the down comforter over her pale chiffon gown—such a dumb thing to be wearing to bed in Scotland, she fumed at herself—and went to huddle beside the window and stare out at the Ness River blacksnaking its calm nightly course through the town.

Sleep like a babe was out of the question, she thought. But then babies were not yet plagued with embarrassment; because babies did nothing to invite embarrassment—among the reasons being they could not care less about the ripple of a muscle along a man's lean jaw. And nothing happened to them when a pair of eyes, gray and rimmed with sooty black, went sharply narrow barely concealing the sudden flare of fire at their centers. What did babies know?

Above all, where was there a baby dumb enough to—damn it, she was crazy, really—to lean over and kiss a man's mouth, *uninvited*, the way she kissed his because of a certain thing she couldn't even describe coming at her from the twitch of his lips?

She clutched the blanket closer around her. It was so cold in the room she could almost see her breath; but she could not climb back into bed. The bed was positively haunted.

Now there were two days to torment herself before

Wednesday at Mrs. Mackay's. Two empty days to *think* about it. Of course there was nothing to do but phone Mrs. Mackay in the morning and tell her she just remembered an engagement or something, anything, and get out of this area as fast as she could. But Julie knew that was sheer nonsense even before the thought was formed. Mrs. Mackay would know she was lying because Julie never did learn how to do it convincingly. Besides...

She rose and paced the little room, trailing the down quilt behind her.

Besides, even if Mrs. Mackay bought her unlikely excuse, and even if she left on the earliest train, and even if she awoke next morning in Edinburgh, or York, or London, or Morocco for that matter, what good would that do? She would still have left behind her the thing that was tormenting her more than all else: the humiliation Ian Fraser had heaped on her.

What was wrong with the guy? What kind of a cold fish was he anyway? Would it have cost him something to respond a little, out of politeness if nothing else, when she kissed him? Surely he couldn't have read *passion* into it? It had been circumspect, really...almost. Why the big drama?

Or was it what she strongly suspected all along, an arrogance that led him to imagine she was dangling before him the prospect of a steamy love affair instead of what it really represented—her intense remorse and guilt for the mess she'd put him in. Anyway, did that appall him so that his lips could only pinch up and sit there, prissily critical? While he sought to save himself from "that sex-crazed American female" and the lengths to which she might go?

A milk truck rattling along Ardross Street alerted Julie that morning had arrived. Beyond her window all was still dark, but impatient with the lost night, she began to dress as if to speed the process along.

At breakfast later, Julie listened politely as Mrs. MacPherson listed for her the several nearby tourist attractions to fill her day. But when she left her house shortly,

Julie wandered at random. One place was as good as the next, in her present mood. And the hospital was really too far for walking...

The hospital? She caught herself up short while crossing Tomnahurich Street, narrowly escaping a lorry bearing down on her. That the thought should occur at all shook her severely. Certainly she hadn't even considered walking or riding or flying or just plain materializing at Raigmore again to see the Man of the Iron Lips! Damn! Though wouldn't he love that! "Back again?" he'd say. "So soon?" Probably pulling his covers up under his chin lest he excite her.

On the other hand... well, wouldn't that be the perfect opportunity to straighten him out about that kiss that seemed to turn his blood to crushed ice? With very little effort, feeling as she did now, she could make Audrey's cool British reserve look like nymphomania. That would be *easy*, and fun, too. She would come dashing in, a woman in a hurry. Barely poking her head through the curtain, she would call out, "Oh, hey, fella, I was just passing by... remembered you were here... how you doing? Well, good, that's great..." Of course, he'd say, "Come on in. Sit beside me," and she'd answer airily, "Dahling, I have such a full schedule today. I can't, really, but maybe I'll see you before I leave."

Again she stopped dead where she stood. Then she spun about so sharply her bright wool scarf arced in the wind. Of all the crazy things to think of doing! To *go* to him for any purpose under the sun, reaffirming in his swollen head that she could not stay away!

And yet was there a better way to show him how little she cared? Why not, after all?

Why *not*? Because he'd see through that like the Seven Veils. Because you don't happen to be passing when you have to take a cab way out of town to get there at all! Because, because... Oh, Julie thought, her mind was fuzzy from hunger. She had to go someplace and eat!

She cleared her head with a shake, tugged her scarlet

Tam a sharp notch down across her ears until her crisp black curls wriggling free barely peeped from under. Then, dark brows lowering, she swung off toward Eden Court and lunch.

The place, a complex of theater, art gallery, restaurant and endless charm, stole her mind briefly from the nagging irritations besetting her. She chose a table beside one of the tall crystal-clear windows overlooking the great lawn that swept to the river, and the stone houses lining its far bank, and she managed to get through most of her cold meat and salad platter before she thought of Ian again. And then it was to wonder why she had not simply considered phoning him to convey what she intended through the chill politeness of her tone.

She would say, "Hello, Ian Fraser? Ah yes, Mrs. Boland here. I just remembered you're still in there, and before I got too involved with business, thought I'd see how you were coming along. Well, isn't that nice? I'm so glad. Oh dear, no, I'm afraid I'll be gone by then . . . couldn't possibly squeeze in a visit."

Okay, what was wrong with that, she thought? Absolutely nothing, and the phones she had noticed were out in the lobby.

She pushed her plate away, preparing to rise, only to sink back weak from the sudden roar of excitement tearing through her veins. It was recalling the sound of his voice that did it, the soft and lovely Scottish sound that managed somehow to dull the edge of his snidest cracks. Even those he'd hurled at her at the peak of that terrible row before the crash. "Gir-rl, have you gone crazy?" Even later, at his hospital bed, "Are you lecturing me again, lass?"

"Lass," she liked that. It fell so smoothly from his lips, like warmed butter; putting her, and *all* women, in their places—several notches below his. But to her horror it was a place she didn't really mind occupying, not much anyway.

It was mad, of course. Even embarrassing. It made her feel strange, and there was no logical explanation for its effect on her. There was only the sound—the soft burry sound of his muted anger—accompanying the challenge of those long gray probing eyes, unsettling her with unclear messages beamed to her own.

Or was she dreaming it all up...and why?

Whatever the answer, she would not go to see Ian Fraser that day. And she would not telephone to hear him. What she would do, if she ever managed to control the tears biting at her lids, she would throw herself with a frenzy into a wild shopping orgy and think it all through tomorrow.

Tomorrow was a disaster. There was the pressure of time to deal with. If she did not see or talk to him before nightfall, there would never be another chance. Next day would take her to Glenshiel, and after that down and away from the Highlands forever. To see him *following* the visit to Mairi Mackay would be to acknowledge that it had been impossible to drive him from her mind, which she hastened to assure herself was not the case; it merely looked that way.

She spent the morning examining and trying on the purchases she had made the previous afternoon. The thick gray Icelandic sweater of a sort she had long coveted. The heathery violet turtleneck that lit up her eyes like springtime—and a scarlet one in the same style. Finally the huge triangle of a shawl in a range of delicate colors that Julie amused herself half the morning counting before she admitted she was merely pushing off a time of decision.

By late afternoon, having walked for miles through a Scottish haze, she finally took herself in hand. Get this over with, J. B., or you won't sleep for a third miserable night in a row! she commanded herself.

And so at last she found a telephone booth—she already had the hospital's number in her handbag—and dialed. She had decided to play it by ear. Depending on how Ian greeted her, she would go to visit him or she would not.

The hospital operator answered, and Julie asked to speak with him. She was so breathless, she had to repeat his name twice over before she was understood. "I-an Fra-ser," she said. "M-may I please—"

She got no further.

"Oh, mum, sorree. Mr. Fraser was discharged yesterday evening."

Well, that was that. And it really wasn't all that important, was it, she rationalized, her hand trembling as she slipped the phone back on its hook.

If it had been, she might have automatically inquired where she could reach him. But she hadn't done that, because . . . well, obviously, some time in the course of those two grueling days, he had ceased to matter so much after all, she consoled herself, leaving the booth.

Glenshiel House was ancient, its ivy-clad stone bulk giving sprawling evidence of centuries of piecemeal construction and change before it was allowed to settle on its great rolling lawn to contemplate its own private loch.

"A wee lochen," Mrs. Mackay's chauffeur called it for Julie's edification when she exclaimed in delight seeing its sparkling surface at play with a peekaboo sun.

"All it lacks is peacocks strutting through the gardens," she said.

"Aye," the chauffeur nodded, "and I can remember seeing them as well. But och, those were different times."

"They must have been," Julie said politely. And today is different from yesterday, she thought. Today again she was all business, having thrown off—almost—that net of despondency that had clung to her in recent days.

She had brought with her this morning a bag with only a single change of clothing, enough for the night and next day. Whatever business might develop here could surely be dealt with in that time. Mairi Mackay was not one, she suspected, to haggle. She would name her price and Julie would take it or leave it.

The chauffeur brought the BMW to a stop before a broad terrace and a set of shallow stone steps that rose to it. As Julie ascended them, the chauffeur carrying her bag, a rosy-cheeked, smiling woman approached from the French doors at her back and hurried forward to greet her.

"Mrs. Mackay is called away for a wee time," she said in lilting accents. "An hour or so it will be. I am Moira Eddington, her housekeeper, and I will show you to your room and bring you tea if you like."

She took the bag from Richard the chauffeur, and Julie followed her into a large and tastefully furnished drawing room where a blazing fire sent friendly welcoming sounds across the great hearth. She exclaimed aloud, "Oh, beautiful," to the housekeeper's pleasure. Her knowledgeable eye estimated at a glance that nearly every item in the room was at least two centuries old. She longed to caress the polished wood of an armoire she passed as Moira guided her toward a circular staircase that led to the upper level. She was already regretting having taken only that single change of clothing. She could have spent weeks here among these treasures.

The floor above split at the upper landing and led in so many directions that Julie giggled. "I'll get lost here. I don't dare leave my room. There are so many doors."

"Ooh, aye," the woman agreed cheerfully. "All guest rooms, and back there is Mrs. Mackay's wing." Then with easy humor, "Give a shout and I'll send a rescue party."

She opened a door at the farthest end of a passageway, and Julie drew in her breath. Clearly Mrs. Mackay had spared little expense, and her taste was impeccable.

But what drew Julie's eye even before the velvet lushness of all the appurtenances was the balcony beyond, and the charming diamond-paned doors that opened out upon it. She hurried there at once, to gaze so long at the "wee lochen" it overlooked that the housekeeper inquired, "Would you like your tea out there, Mrs. Boland? Though you'll need a jumper or a shawl, for it's very chilly and the wind is rising."

Julie could not forgo the chance, though the sky was a lowering gray now, the sun having had its play for the day. "Oh yes," she answered, "I'll bundle up. That would be a delight, Moira. Thank you so much."

In spite of the clouds scudding before the roughening winds, the threat of rain seemed hardly imminent, and when Moira had returned with the promised tea, Julie luxuriated as never before in her life. Consuming quantities of sliver-thin cucumber sandwiches that the housekeeper had heaped on the triple-tiered tray along with warm scones and raspberry jam, Julie managed to all but empty the silver teapot. She thought she had never eaten so elegantly before, and that she could very easily be spoiled by such service and never want to leave.

She rose and stretched at last, hugging about her the new wool shawl she had purchased in Inverness the day before. The wind was sharper now. Wandering along the terrace, she realized that it actually extended for the breadth of this entire wing. And that hers was not the only room to open out onto it. As she followed it to its end, she counted six sets of identical doors—a charming arrangement for groups of houseguests, she thought—and in that moment, the skies opened up. She had had plenty of warning, but could not bring herself to go inside. Now the first spatter of rain turned to ropes and sheets hurtling from the clouds. In seconds she was drenched, her hair and cheeks awash. Her wool shawl grew so heavy with water, she dropped it on a chair rather than drag it dripping into her room. The silk blouse she wore beneath it, already sopping, clung and flattened against her skin.

Fleeing for cover, she found the door and grasped its knob, pulling hard against the battering wind—the same that sent her pell-mell over the threshold to the murkiness within. A second too late she saw that the room was not her own.

Gasping, clearing the water from her eyes and ears, she stood there—suddenly stupefied.

"And have you never learned to knock, lass? Don't they teach you manners over there?"

CHAPTER SIX

HE LAY SPRAWLED upon his back, his protruding cast partially obscuring her view of him. Visible was his chest, bared except for a surgical tape binding his rib cage. In the ruddy flicker from the hearth his skin gleamed smooth and bronzed.

This much she saw at first gasp along with the mound of covers on the floor beside his bed. And those long, gray, dark-lashed eyes raging at the intrusion. Her own leveled with his face, not daring to wander and risk lingering too openly on the breadth of his shoulders, or the play of his knotting muscles.

Recovering from first shock, she might have voiced a hasty, "Excuse me," and fled into the rain. But his inference that she had known very well what she was doing demanded an immediate retort.

Her mind was too disordered to connect all the scathing responses flooding it and shape them into one searing answer. She stood rigid, dripping on his rug, her hands unwittingly kneading the wet silk of her blouse where it cleaved to her quivering breasts. She saw his gaze drop and rivet there, boldly. Realizing, she folded her arms across her chest and glared her contempt of him.

"Are you—thinking—" she began, faltering from agitation, "that you're so irresistible—that I would wait outside that door for a handy storm to blow me into your room so I can—*rhapsodize* and—and *drool* over your body? *Relax!* My six-year old nephew is more interesting!"

His jaw sagged, but she gave him no chance to respond.

"You hear me out!" She moved in closer, her shaking hand sweeping her thick damp curls off her face where they promptly bounced back; meanwhile ignoring his futile efforts to draw the sheet that had caught around his cast over the rest of him. She saw that the effort was painful, but felt no pity. "I'm a married woman," she reminded him. "I know what nude men look like, and yes, I can be turned on. But never—*never* by an overblown ego! That it even crossed your mind that I deliberately came looking for you is contemptible arrogance. I had no idea whatever that you were here at Glenshiel. And if I had, bet on it, I'd have declined Mrs. Mackay's invitation before she got it all said."

"All right, gir-rl, now you hear me out," he began when she seemed to have run out of steam. (And there it was, that blurry softness again.) "Don't you go thinking *I* arranged things this way for the chance of exhibiting myself to you. Being here was no idea of mine. It's too close to Audrey, is what it is, her not three miles across the mountain."

"That is *your* problem, Ian. Why take it out on me?"

"Aye, well, I'm steaming about it proper. My gran takes over everybody's life like it were her own. I wanted back in my croft. I got all the help I need. She's an interfering woman. All women are interfering—"

He was fighting the tangled covers as he ranted, half to

himself, tugging at them futilely until it got on Julie's nerves.

"Oh, shut up a minute. Here," she cut in on his tirade. Coming to his side, she reached, and in a single movement tossed the obstreperous flannel sheet over his naked leanness, making no effort to see or not to see. Bending across him, she tucked a corner beneath his shoulder, much as any nurse would have done.

Abruptly she stood erect and looked away. Those brief seconds of closeness to him had struck like a warm sea wave. She started wordlessly for the door, aware that her cheeks burned pink and that the last thing she needed was for him to see.

"Come back, you didn't finish," he called after her. "Lift it off the cast, will you now? It feels hot enough to melt."

She turned to him again and did as he asked, arranging the sheet above his knee and wishing the throb at the hollow of her throat would slow down and cease.

He wasn't satisfied. It wasn't good enough. Grumbling, he yanked the sheet higher, exposing a length of dark muscular thigh. The throb sounded again, so loud in her ears she wondered if he caught the echo. She longed to escape but her legs felt weak.

His voice came to her, thinly, across her heart's pounding. It was gruff, but sheepish too, she thought.

"It wasn't you I was raging at," he muttered, leaning back on his pillow. She saw the way his rumpled hair made shaggy clumps all over his head, and for an instant hated herself for almost reaching out to smooth it for him. It added ice to her reply.

"Quite all right. I've seen better tantrums from the six-year-old."

"Him again," he rumbled. "It's only that I'm lying here helpless, and Gran's mapping out my future, and I damn well don't like it. Here, come closer. Sit and talk if you like—"

Julie had a fleeting recall of that last time she had sat and talked. She half turned to him, speaking with a little tremor, "No, sorry. I have to change my clothes. I'm wet."

"Aye, I noticed." His glance roamed again overtly to the peachy glow where the wet silk still clung to her breasts, and there was no way to stifle their rise and fall, or the thrum, thrum, thrum beneath them. She felt a slow flush rise from deep in their cleavage, warming her like wine. Warming the white flesh of her throat, and then her cheeks, even to the roots of her hair. She felt herself weaving again on her feet and pressed a hand to her heart to steady it. His voice came to her distantly. "Stand by the fire, then. You'll soon be dry." It sounded like a whisper in her ears. She wondered if that was the way he had meant it.

"N-no," she breathed, and could not be aware of the shine in her eyes saying it, while wanting suddenly to say, "Yes, why not? Of course." Wanting with such yearning in that moment, if she did not go at once, she knew she would not be able. The feel of his eyes on her held her, as if she were bound to his bed.

His look was inscrutable—as inscrutable, it struck her, as his mouth when she had kissed him. She divined nothing from it now, just as then she had divined nothing from the deadness of his lips. She stood torn and wavering.

"Oh, sit, lass," he said, and it was almost a plea. "Here, toss that dressing gown over your shoulders—"

She could not believe she was doing it. She seemed to be standing off in another consciousness, watching herself drawing his wool robe around her, aware of an aroma that already she had come to associate with him. Then she edged to the bed, and sat there. There was no chair close by, or she would have taken it. Nevertheless she perched— flushed, her strawberry lips moist and slightly parted—but at a prim enough distance, her back rigidly erect.

She was sitting there exactly so, moments after, when voices could be heard rising up from the stairwell, and drawing closer.

"Your grandmother is back," she said hastily. "I'll go."

"It's not my Gran. It's Moira," he answered edgily, "and herself—Audrey. Gran should have warded her off instead of going traipsing somewhere."

"Then I'll leave."

"Stay," he said. She wondered at the sudden hardness of his mouth, the muscles working in his cheeks.

"I can't. I must go," she said.

"No, stay," he repeated more firmly, and as she made to rise, his hand locked on her wrist. "I'm asking you. I'm wanting it, Julie." There was urgency, even command, in his tone.

"What are you doing? Let me go, Ian, I want to get out of here," she protested. The voices had reached the head of the stairs, only yards down the hall. His hold on her strengthened like thin bands of steel, hurting her. "Ian, *stop!*"

"Julie, don't go. I want you here now." His words were clipped off short, and though directed at her, his mind seemed clearly on the approaching visit. He gave a swift little tug that brought her falling upon him, angry now. For it broke over her like a cold shower why he wanted her there now: an intimate scene for Audrey Grant to walk in upon—and hopefully walk out of his life forever.

She was aghast at his gall. Then abruptly, no less aghast at the struggle flaring within herself—her mind, *her body*. Lying across him, straining still, she could feel the hardness of him, every protrusion pressing into her soft flesh. No matter the sheet divided them. It seemed gossamer thin, even crazily provocative.

It was over in a twinkling, but he had dared to fill every split instant of it. His big hard hands had restrained her, roughly—then gently, and fierce again. Deep within her a well of fire leaped, surging to him in a single frenetic moment.

Then because he had to—because she fought him, and more likely because his rib cage was tearing at him with pain, he released her. Drained, limp, she pulled torturously away from his arms, seething, "How—dare—you?"

"Och, admit it," she heard him compound his impudence, "it wasn't all bad, was it? Come, lass, give us a kiss now, will you not?"

With a resounding swat to his cheek, she thrust him off.

"I'll not be used by you, Ian Fraser, for your nasty little games. Damned if I know what that girl sees in you!"

He wasn't listening. He had pulled the sheet over his head pretending sleep, and Julie whirled from him in disgust. "I'm sorry for her," she tossed back on her way to the terrace. "I wouldn't have you at the end of a ten-foot pole."

"I don't remember offering you, lass," rose muffled from the sheet.

She slammed the door on that and found her way through the waning storm to her room, where three times at least as she slipped into dry clothes, she had to dash the tears from her eyes.

And why? she demanded of herself. Was he worth tears, too? He was the most irritating of men. In a span of thirty seconds he could infuriate her, then charm her, then send her into a screaming rage. And it was mad, considering he was nothing in her life, and this was no personal issue between them. It had nothing to do with *them*—him and her. It was that annoying male prerogative he automatically appropriated for himself—much as Gary had, come to think of it—all the rights, all the privileges.

First he had used Audrey, very likely talking her into his bed with him. Then, no doubt tiring of her before the wedding, he wanted rid of her. And *now* he blithely expected to use Julie herself against the girl. Oh, sure, she could just see herself in a torrid embrace with Ian Fraser for his convenience, just as Audrey walked through his door!

As for what happened back there on his bed, *nothing* happened—of any significance, anyway. She was not going to labor under any guilt for that. He was an absolute *dog*, daring to pass his hands over her against her will. She had never claimed to be invulnerable. But *he* had started it, and he was fairly expert at it, too.

Presently, hearing the muffled dialogue between him and Audrey beyond the wall, she hadn't the slightest doubt it was that "expertness" of his that had brought them to where they were right now.

It was a nuisance having to listen to them; she wished Mrs. Mackay had had the foresight to assign her to another room, instead of this one smack up against his wall. It was of such a thickness that it rendered words unintelligible while allowing their emotions to filter through.

Audrey's monotone went on a bit overlong, Julie thought, and she wondered if Ian was still under his sheet. Then came some rumbling answer, and abruptly a lion's bellow, as if disturbed over a haunch of deer. Audrey again, her thin, high-pitched wail broken by tears. So the girl *could* cry. Would she ever learn he was not worth tears? He was an egocentric hit-and-run lover which that poor kid over there was just finding out.

She had begun to collect her wet garments when a light tap at her door drew her around.

"Mrs. Boland?"

"Oh yes, come," Julie called a trifle breathlessly, and Mairi Mackay entered, apologizing at once.

"I'm sorry to have been away when you arrived. I'd received a message about old Mrs. Colquhoun at Balnain being ill, and there is no telephone, so I hurried over. It's a bit of a distance but there must have been a mistake because she was fine and had no idea what it was all about.

"Oh, that poor lad Ben Farquhar it was who came to tell me about it. He's a dear child, but he is retarded. Probably got it all wrong. Nevertheless, I hope Moira had made you comfortable. And oh, my dear, all your wet things—"

Julie laughed nervously. "Yes, I must hang them somewhere. I got drenched in the shower, right there on your terrace. It was so sudden. I couldn't find my door—"

"Ah, yes. Well, give them to me, I'll have Moira take care of them." As she spoke, Mrs. Mackay took them from Julie's hand, one by one, her skirt, the silk blouse, and the heavy wool shawl retrieved as she'd scurried back earlier.

"Thank you," Julie said, but Mrs. Mackay's gaze had traveled deeper into the room.

"There's another, I believe," she said, and Julie, following her look, saw that other, draped on a chair where she had dropped it. Ian's dressing gown that in her angry rush to be gone she had forgotten to leave behind.

Her eyes grazed her hostess's and she murmured, "It's

not very wet, really." But her cheeks flamed and she writhed with the need to explain, and the lack of words to explain with. At length she murmured, "As I said, I couldn't find my own door—and—I really had no idea he was there, Mrs. Mackay."

"Of course," Mrs. Mackay answered, and Julie thought irritably, Hurrah for British cool. "I'll take it along, if I may," she added. "And—ah, did you have a pleasant visit?"

The black eyes fixed on Julie's with such tenacity it seemed they could never be torn loose unless she replied.

"I wasn't with him very long. I left when I—when we heard his fiancée approaching—" She stopped, her color deepening even further. She had made it sound so much worse than it was. But Mrs. Mackay appeared not to notice. Her brows knitted ever so slightly in a hint of a frown.

"I would have preferred," she said as if addressing herself, "if Audrey had waited and not come by today. I told her earlier on the phone that it wasn't a good idea. If I'd not been called away, I'd have—uh, prevented it. I didn't think Moira would have allowed her up there. Audrey's a sweet child, but sometimes a little headstrong, I fear. And, Moira, I'm afraid, is much too romantic."

All the time she spoke, she was carefully folding the damp garments, handling them abstractly, dropping those confidences from her lips as if Julie were not present. Beyond the wall the sounds had all but ceased, except for an intermittent rumble or wail. And once, clearly, a sob, at which Mrs. Mackay shook her head.

"She upsets him, so," she said half under her breath. "A pity she doesn't realize—"

Julie suppressed a scream. So the poor jilted kid in there upset *him*! Didn't Mairi give even a teensy thought to how he had upset her? For whatever silly lovers' quarrel they might have had...

But she could not say this to Mairi Mackay. She was a guest in her home. All she could rightfully tell her was that she was quite anxious to be on with the business that had brought her to Glenshiel so that she could be away.

Mairi Mackay looked at her when that was said as if she

could not recall what business it *was* that had brought Julie
to her home. And then, "Oh, yes, the old pieces. Yes, of
course. Tomorrow is time enough, surely. Shall we go down
first for some sherry, my dear?"

Julie wanted to decline, to ask to have it over with sooner,
but she had slipped already under the woman's unyielding
dominance. She grasped at a straw. "I'm afraid I didn't
bring any other clothes along."

"Why not, Mrs. Boland?" Mairi Mackay chided mildly
as she drew Julie toward the door.

"I—hadn't intended—"

Mairi Mackay was not listening. In the passageway she
excused herself a moment and walking off a few paces,
tapped with her light, but peremptory tap on Ian's room.
The voices within sheared off at once, and Mrs. Mackay
pushed the door open and, to Julie's horror, announced,
"Ian, Mrs. Boland is returning your dressing gown. Oh,
Audrey, how nice to see you. I hope you're feeling better."

The only response was the shocked silence from within,
and Mrs. Mackay did not wait for more. Without another
word she closed Ian's door and rejoined her guest at the
stairhead.

Julie descended beside her speculating on the woman's
thoughtlessness. She was so unfeeling. Julie wondered if
she realized—

She cast a sidelong glance at Mairi Mackay, at the forward tilt of her chin, and the faintest of smiles rimming her
lips with steel, and echoed herself, incredulously this time,
I wonder if she realized . . .

CHAPTER SEVEN

"WILL YOU JOIN us for a sherry, Audrey?"

Mairi Mackay reached for the carafe as she spoke and Julie glanced behind her, startled. The girl had made her descent so noiselessly she might have passed on out of doors unnoticed if Mrs. Mackay had been facing the other way.

"I think not, Mairi," Audrey answered her. "Thank you very much." She spoke in a thin, girlish tone, not yet free of tears. Julie's heart reached out to her. She had been treated abominably, and now, Mrs. Mackay for some obscure reason, was being anything but helpful or comforting. It seemed to Julie, considering her grandson's behavior, that the least she could do was to lavish some affection and understanding on her.

Audrey added with a gentle smile, "I really have to get

back to father. He's still—*very* upset. He says it is fortunate
poor Mum didn't live to see this."

"Of course," Mrs. Mackay agreed, and Julie winced.
"And I am so sorry I wasn't at home when you came by.
But do you know, Audrey, the strangest thing happened.
Young Ben Farquhar came to tell me Mrs. Colquhoun at
Balnain was suddenly taken with something dreadful. I
really couldn't make it out, but you know the poor child.
So I rushed straight over—Alec had to take me in the van
because, of course, Richard had gone for Mrs. Boland. But
when I got there, there wasn't a thing wrong with Mrs.
Colquhoun, and she didn't seem to know anything about
it. I thought it very odd. Don't you, Audrey?"

Julie could not imagine why she was going on about it
when Audrey clearly wanted nothing more than to escape.
But she had pinned the girl with her eyes, and Audrey
waited with the politeness the well-reared young practice
toward their garrulous elders. Then, seeing Mrs. Mackay
finished, she shook her head and murmured, "Yes, quite
strange, Mairi." And, "If you'll excuse me . . ."

"Of course, my dear."

"Oh," Audrey seemed to remember something. "Mrs.
Boland, forgive me, I was very preoccupied. But Ian asked
me to thank you for returning his dressing gown."

Julie's eyes hit hard at the girl, then quickly fell away.
But Audrey's were wide and totally innocent of ulterior
motive, as if the incident had left no special impression on
her.

Then she was gone and Mairi Mackay, refilling Julie's
glass, remarked as if there had been no interruption, "You
mentioned, I believe, that you brought no other clothing,
Mrs. Boland?"

"That's true. Just these I'm wearing now. I hadn't expected to need them until tomorrow when I really must be
leaving."

"Oh, too bad. So soon. I could not possibly get at the
pieces I wanted you to see in such a short time. They're
stored up there, you see," with a wave in the general di-

rection of the upper stories, "and some are even crated. I was planning to ask Richard, and Gordon my gardener, to climb up there and uncover the things. But that would be late tomorrow at best when Gordon returns from Aberdeen. There's been a family funeral there. However, I know what we can do, yes." All enthusiasm now. "I shall have Richard pick up your things at Maggie MacPherson's. I'll phone Maggie and she'll have them ready. Oh, no trouble at all, my dear. Richard has to go to town anyway. Ian's wheelchair is to be delivered at the depot. He'll take the van and do it all in one trip."

She must have caught the look of speechless astonishment on Julie's face, but it did not deter her. Julie's mind raced. No way, she thought, was she going to let Mairi Mackay run her affairs, too. She couldn't believe this woman! She just took over. Julie started to protest, but Mrs. Mackay was already off on her mission.

Before the dinner hour Richard returned with her clothes and the wheelchair that Mrs. Mackay had acquired for Ian's use. She had taken it to him herself, and a big unwieldy thing it looked. But alone she had shoved it into a lift that, as she explained to Julie with a triumphant smile, her late husband had had installed at *her* instigation when he developed difficulty walking. "He opposed it, of course," she pointed out, "but I insisted."

Julie had a flashing impression of the late Mr. Mackay "opposing" anything Mairi instigated, and her sympathies flowed to him in his grave.

"Now what would I ever have done without it?" his widow wondered aloud as the lift door clacked shut on her. And just in time, Julie thought, having suppressed a burning urge to answer, "Why, then, you might have left Ian to his own devices in his croft on his own land that he's so anxious to get back to." She waited until she heard Mrs. Mackay leave the lift and enter Ian's room. Then she took the stairs to her own where Richard followed soon after with her bags.

"Will that be all, mum?"

"Yes, thank you so much, Richard," she said, glaring at the bags as if it were their fault they had arrived.

"Then I will go and help Madam with young Mr. Fraser." It was the last civil word spoken in that hour.

It started with a roar—gorillalike, Julie thought.

"I will not get into that old man's trolley. *Not*—you hear that, Gran?"

"Of course, you will, my dear. Now be a good lad and let Richard help you."

"Gran, I'm warning you," he bellowed. "I like Richard and I don't want to hurt him. But if he tries, I give you my word I shall belt him."

"Of course you won't, my dear," Mairi answered without a ripple. "You'll relax and allow us both to transfer you to this nice seat."

"Back, Gran, back!" he shouted. "If you get hurt in the struggle, don't say I didn't warn you. Now away with you."

"But you can't spend all your days cooped up here like this, darling. It's too depressing."

"Aye, and who brought me here?" he yelled. "My croft's my own. My men know my habits. They'd do for me—"

"Your men are away on the land all day with the harvest and the sheep to look after. And their own wives and children to go home to at night. You know quite well there is no time for them to be nursing you."

"There are the girls."

"Oh, yes, I daresay, the young girls. But really, Ian, they are *young girls*." The implication was clear enough. "And it's too much to ask—"

"*I'll* say what's too much. Gran, if it weren't for your interfering—it's a terrible habit you have—poking your Mackay nose into everyone's affairs whether or not you're asked. Turning over everybody's applecarts for them, taking hold of their lives like it was your right."

His voice spiraled to such a pitch that Julie bolted into the hall and inched closer to his door, to lend her strength if he grew violent. Richard was a little man, no longer young, and Mrs. Mackay an aging woman. It might well take the three of them to handle Ian, cast, taped rib, and all.

She thought his voice would give out, but there was no end. Then somehow it was herself he was raving about, and she tensed, eavesdropping.

"That American, she's another like yourself—a pushy, interfering woman, the worst kind they make over there. And now she's here and just the other side of the wall, likely spying on me. Why'd you put her there if you had to bring her at all."

"Hush," Mairi ordered him, "you know perfectly well the other guest rooms haven't been used in years. What a silly lad you are."

"You're taunting me, you are. Talking like I'm a kid. Why'd you bring her here, eh? To tell me what to do when you've run out of ideas? Is that it, Gran? Here I lie wracked in pain and you bring in that woman, the very one that brought all this on my head. If it weren't for her, I'd be gone, far from here. And with no damned cast on my leg. Know where I'd be?"

"*No. Tell us*—where?" Julie spoke from the open door leaning on the frame, her tone, her stance, her narrowed eyes heaping ridicule upon him until it overflowed and filled every corner of the room. She saw his mouth open and shut and open again, soundlessly. She moved into the room with measured steps until she stood at the foot of his bed. "Tell us where, go on," she repeated, deceptively low, holding his eyes with her own. She was dimly aware of the others backing out, presumably, she thought, because Mairi Mackay would not wish her chauffeur to witness whatever might follow. Presumably, too, because Mairi might be entertaining some hope that she, a stranger, could better silence her "silly lad." Mairi certainly did treat him as though he were young. And that, Julie knew for a fact, would get her nowhere.

"You were saying?" she prompted. "You would be where if I hadn't stopped you?"

He was not to be cowed. He answered, though without

shouting, she noticed. "I'd be away from all this for sure, if it's any of your prying affair."

She ignored the slur. "I'll tell you exactly where you'd be, Ian Fraser. You'd be away, all right, skulking around the countryside, too ashamed to go home. Because a man—a real man doesn't put a girl through what you did to Audrey Grant."

"You know nothing about it, lass."

"Only what you told me. You fell out of love on your wedding morning. *On your wedding morning, man!* You decided to hit the road because, like trillions of bridegrooms before you, you got cold feet. And so you turned coward, and sold your honor for—a broken leg! Ha!"

"*Shut up*, Julie." But he did not yell it. His voice shook, but Julie was certain it could not be heard beyond the door that Mairi had shut behind her. "I'm warning you—"

"Don't use that threat on me, Ian. It won't work. I'm not afraid of you even without your cast. I'm a pushy, interfering woman, remember?" She was enjoying herself now.

"You've got no honor yourself, lass. You're an eavesdropper or you wouldn't have heard that."

"They'd have heard you in the Western Isles, the way you were shouting, and about me, at that."

"And why not? You're conspiring against me, you've been conspiring ever since I met you."

"Conspiring? Me? How and why, for heaven's sake?"

"How and why? To get the wedding back on the rails, that's how and why."

"It's no affair of mine, Ian. But if you ask me—"

"Which I don't—"

"It's time that wedding did get back on the rails, with you aboard, real soon. Surely the whole glen is talking. Clan wars must have been fought for less. Like it or not, it doesn't reflect any glory on you, and if honor still means anything, you'll never live it down. Still, as I said, that's your problem. Now give me one good reason, other than pity for Audrey, that I would give a damn."

"Here it comes, lass: *Because your husband left you and*

*you've got it in for any man that'll ever walk away from
a girl! Am I right?"*

It was a low blow and it bowled her over. She had
forgotten that he knew. But he'd dredged it up out of his
own cynical anger and twisted it to suit himself. She said,
"Touché!" and saw the satisfaction in his eyes. But he was
not finished.

"Want another good reason? Because you're paying me
back for not taking advantage of you." His eyes suddenly
danced.

"That is . . . sick!" Her fury soared as laughter leaped
from his throat.

"And for not kissing you back as you wanted at the
hospital, lass." The blood surged to her face. "Aye, I knew
how you felt, but that wasn't all. *You* knew how you felt,
and it's been telling on you ever since."

She had no breath to speak. He'd turned the tables so
deftly he'd left her floundering.

"Save yourself the trouble, lass. I won't hold your shame-
less behavior against you, coming to my room the way you
did, all wet from the rain and charming. And of course, you
wouldn't kiss me when I wanted—knowing you'd hang on
too long, not wishing to let me go, and Audrey coming in
upon us."

He's having a ball, she thought, tears biting at her lids.
He's relishing every blooming minute of it, lying there with
that ridiculous cast and that vengeful smile on his lips.

He was wearing pajama tops this time, but his fingers
were busy opening their buttons as he teased with his ad-
olescent humor. He saw her eyes following his movements
and chuckled.

"That's just so you don't tear them off me, lass, in your
passion." He was laughing so hard he could just form the
words. In a moment she would leave him. But first she
wanted that one devastating "last word" to leave him *with*!
She wanted him to know how low he stood with her; something was on the tip of her tongue. Then abruptly her face
was full of pillow!

He'd flung it at her, roaring with laughter and she gasped

and a second later, buried him in it.

She had swung around to the side of the bed to do it, pounding him with it over and over until he seized it from her and hurled it again. She ducked, laughing aloud as it struck the wall behind her. Retrieving it, she scored with a perfect shot. He was too quick. He'd already sent another flying that caught her unaware. She collapsed in laughter. In moments the room was alive with flying pillows, she sending them back as fast as he launched them. Then he launched one too many, grabbed at his rib cage, and groaned.

"Oh, God," she gasped, springing to him. "Did you—do something?"

His face was screwed up in pain as she hovered anxiously. But his breathing eased in moments and she murmured, "I'm so sorry. I shouldn't have let it go on."

He lay back with a deep sigh and reached for her hand. "Tell me about it, lass," he said.

A bubble of laughter that was pure relief rose in her throat, but she suppressed it. "That was a silly thing to be doing, wasn't it, Ian?"

"I don't know. It was fun," he answered low.

"But—"

"No 'buts,' it was fun." His voice had dropped to a level new to her. His eyes, narrowed again, seemed alive and dark with meaning. His hand curled tightly around hers, and she made no effort to change that. She could not think of a single good reason to do so. She let it lie there, and stared at it, her breath escaping through her parted lips in warm little wisps. Something kept throbbing and pounding in her throat; he could not possibly miss seeing it.

He was watching her still, intently, his eyes shadowed by a thick fall of hair. The reddish glints in the sandy gold of it dancing in the lamplight drew her. Her hands longed for a moment to plunge among its tangled strands and bury themselves there.

Even before he whispered it, she knew it was coming. "Bend to me, lass. Kiss me..."

She closed her eyes. The last time he had said that, here on this very bed, earlier on this very day, she had hit him. She could not remember at this moment precisely why.

"Lass..."

She smiled. He was watching her through slitted eyes that seemed so intent on her face she could have touched the place they burned. She studied his lips. Yes, again she wanted to touch them with her fingers, and bend to him as he asked, and kiss him...

"Julie, can't we finish what you started—there at the hospital?"

With a breathy sigh her mouth fell to his. A moment it smoldered there, ripples of flame racing between them. With dizzying abruptness he seized and dragged her to him, urging his body to her soft, firm breast. A low groan escaped him and his arms tightened about her with a violence that rocked her senses. She drew back, feeling faint, and heard distantly, *"Julie, my God!"*

His lips sought hers with new urgency, forcing them to part, exploring, and toying and playing with them, devouring and bruising them, awakening little cries in her throat, of pain, and pleasure, all intermingled, until suddenly it was over.

He fell back on his pillow, his chest heaving with deep, shuddering breaths. Julie lay beside him now, her reeling head on his shoulder, though she remembered nothing of having slipped to that warm and intimate place. She knew only that her lips were pained and she wished that particular pain would never stop. Then she remembered she was lying in Ian Fraser's bed, and her hand, investigating, found that her blouse was fallen half open and that she would never have undone the small pearl buttons herself, and that they were too secure to have come apart on their own, and somehow in the tussle, Ian had managed. Smoothly. And cleverly, she thought. Like a man who knew his way around pearl buttons.

Now that her head was clearing, she remembered with an electrifying shock that she was not wearing a bra. She had removed her wet one earlier and had not had a chance to replace it from the fresh clothes Richard had brought her.

She struggled furtively to work the buttons into their holes without Ian sensing, and calling attention to what she was already wanting to forget. Whatever possessed her, she wondered, genuinely at odds with herself. She still barely knew him—less than a week. And there she lay in bed beside him. Worse, she was straining already to forget the feel of his body on hers. And his hands that had evoked a fever that even Gary, her own husband, had never communicated. (Strange, how she used to believe that was it, that was the best there was.) What in heaven's dear name was she allowing to happen to herself? Was it plain raw sex she was missing?

"Let me do it for you, lass. You're wearing your fingers to the bone."

"Go away." She shook his hand from her and sat upright.

But without ceremony, he reached for her shoulders and forced her back until his face hung above hers again. His eyes plunged deep, deep into hers that were pools of sudden fear—fear not of him. Of herself. If he were to touch her again...

His eyes knew her secret, as if it were written large on her forehead. Her face burned.

"What are you afraid of, lass? Didn't you like it—as far as it went?"

"Stop it, Ian," she said, but made no move to rise from him.

"Stop what? I won't rape you, lass. It's not my way. I'm not asking it now, anyway. I've never done it with a cast on my leg, and the rib isn't easy yet. And I would hate to disappoint you. Besides I like a lass that'll come to me, wanting me."

She bit her lip. "You'll wait a long time," she said. "Until you're so old, you'll forget what you had in mind."

He laughed softly, his fingers playing with a tendril of her hair. "I doubt it. Aye, it'll be sooner than you're admitting. You didn't fight me off, Julie. You liked it."

"Stop it, Ian. All right...it was...fun. And it's over,

and it should never have happened. Like it or not, there is still Audrey, and there is a lot of rectifying you have to do. And suddenly, I'm quite frankly ashamed I let this happen."

"Ay, Audrey—still," he drawled lazily.

"It's not funny, Ian. You'd better start thinking very seriously about it. It's not going to go away."

"Unfortunately," he agreed. Then with a throaty chuckle, he queried, "But after sampling it, lass, would you be wasting such talent on Miss Audrey Grant?"

She sat up again, her back to him, finishing closing the buttons as she spoke. "There's no need whatsover, Ian, to keep reminding me that I reacted as any woman would who'd had an ample share of sex in her life and suddenly it was snatched away." Her words fell in a rapid stream. She did not look behind her. She wanted it all out, and she did not want to be diverted. "Don't go charging it up to your superlative sexual prowess, my good man. It just might be that you're a man and I'm a woman, and we're like two ships passing in the night, and—and tooting our horns at each other. But it doesn't mean one of us is going to make a U-turn in the middle of the ocean and keep on tooting together! Besides—" She turned now to meet his eyes. They were dark and serious, all the humor drained from them.

"Besides, what?"

"I happen to be on Audrey's side. I think she's had a raw and rotten deal, and she'll have to live with that in this little tight glen all her life: the girl whom the laird jilted!"

"And so you want me to marry her, do you?"

"I want you to do the right thing. If you're half a man, you will. If you loved her enough once to ask her to marry you, you'll love her again, and—bet on it, Ian, your feet will warm up in bed along with the rest of you."

His hands were behind his head. His gaze had not left her face, and it unsettled her a little.

"Aye," he said, "and then you would write me down in your little black book as a good lad, and half a man, eh? And *then* would you be willing to come to bed with the other half?"

Her breath pulled in sharply. She shook her head, at a

complete loss for words; until in a burst of outrage she cried,
"Wh-what do you take me for?"

"A liar," he answered readily. "And a priggish one at
that." His voice had dropped to a disturbingly low pitch,
and though his hand crept up losing itself in the wild disorder
of her hair, she did not move; not even when the tips of his
fingers brushed her ear and trembled there a moment. And
traced a warm trail down her cheek to her throat, and deeper,
easily manipulating the first few buttons of her blouse. She
seemed mesmerized. She shuddered only when she felt his
touch upon the soft, yielding flesh beneath the silk. Then
she drew away, the spell breaking, and heard his voice
emerging from a humming in her ears.

"Ah yes, you can give me all that fine advice even after
kissing me the way you did. Julie, I'm no school lad. I've
kissed and been kissed. I've held women in my arms and
been held in theirs. I've felt the blood roar in my veins,
and I've known when theirs did, too. I know a woman's
breathing. I know her gasping. I know her sighing and the
little sounds escaping her when she least knows it. And
when her body is ripe and ready and surging to mine, *I
know that, too*. And never have I felt it as I felt yours. You
want me, Julie, the way that I want you."

A sob springing from her throat startled her. He reached
for her again, but she flung out an arm, thrusting him off.

"Stop it. You're off on an ego trip again. You're not all
that great."

"Still a liar," he said, his eyes slitting, but an exultant
light glistening in them, like smoldering bonfires, infuri-
ating her.

"You and all those women you've kissed and fondled
and slept with!" She sobbed. "And your disgusting male
comparisons—as if we're all breeding mares? What are you
trying to prove, Ian? Why did we have to go through this
whole crazy dialogue? I didn't come in here for—*this*!"

She was on her feet, glaring at him through the tears that
would not stop flowing. She saw him lift himself on an
elbow, but was not fast enough to escape as he seized her
wrist in a viselike grip. He paid no heed to her struggles

and held her easily, watching and waiting almost patiently until she grew silent and ceased to resist. It was then that he answered her.

"No, lass. You didn't come for 'this.' But neither did you fly from it. And I did not hear you cry out to be saved when it was so warm between us on this bed. Now will you lie once more and deny it?"

Then he flung her hand off and watched as she stumbled toward the door.

CHAPTER EIGHT

A GONG from below brought her up tense before she reached the door to Ian's room. She froze, uncertain, until he said, "It's the dinner bell."

"Oh," she murmured and continued to the door. But he stopped her.

"Aye, I'll go down now. If you'll roll that blasted chair to the bed, I shall get into it. Suddenly I have an appetite."

Roll it yourself, she longed to say. But she turned, nevertheless, and did as he asked. He was, after all, helpless. Though not so helpless as to forget to cling to her needlessly as she assisted him from bed to chair. For a humiliating instant her face was a scant inch from Ian's, her view of him blocked by his hair falling softly across her eyes. She could feel the warmth of his breath on her cheek and her glance darted off nervously to the far wall.

Following so swiftly on the heels of their tempestuous clash, such contact was annoyingly unnatural. His low laugh, which he took no pains to muffle, sent such a shaft of rage through her, she barely resisted dropping him, cast, taped rib cage and all. Mocking her while she was helping him was intolerable!

The maneuver done with, she guided the chair through the door and to the lift where, thankfully, she saw Richard waiting to assist. She walked off then, her eyes straight before her, and disappeared into her room.

She would have preferred to have a tray sent up, but did not dare request it. She would also have preferred some straight talk with Mrs. Mackay as to when they could get at those pieces she had come to view. She had a feeling the matter was of less importance to Mairi Mackay than to herself and she would have difficulty pinning the woman down.

Brooding, she changed, burying the despicable pearl-buttoned blouse at the bottom of her bag and selecting a soft little dress of a shadowy azalea pink, largely because it was the first garment out of her bag. She did not see it as flattering, forgetting that when she had bought it on a spree at Bloomingdale's in New York, she had not missed the glow the color brought to her petal smooth skin or the violet it made of her eyes.

She was not looking for "flattering" at this point. She merely longed for the dinner to be over, and after a decent interval, to return to her room.

Downstairs she quailed before Mairi Mackay's approval. "My dear, you look enchanting," she announced, then added in a hasty whisper, "However did you get him into that chair?"

Julie allowed a smile. "I was 'pushy' and 'interfering,' what else?" she said, and did not care if Ian heard. Mrs. Mackay, to her surprise, giggled.

At dinner she was seated across from him, but she kept her eyes down and made no effort to initiate small talk. She did extract from her hostess a promise to send her men servants to the upper reaches of the house and uncover certain items for her to see in the morning.

"Especially that table, you know, the thirteenth-century table, Mrs. Mackay. I'm very anxious—"

"Of course," came her reply. "But you must take full advantage while you're here, Mrs. Boland, and enjoy the surroundings. Do you ride?"

Julie did indeed ride. She had spent much of her early youth exploring the pine barrens and the beach bordering the Sound astride her very own horse.

"You're most welcome, then," Mrs. Mackay told her. "It will take the men awhile to collect and polish the things up there. Meanwhile, there's a lovely trail to be ridden through our forest. Several trails in fact. And Heather is a gentle mare, and knows them all. Now if the weather cooperates . . ."

The weather more than cooperated. After a night of wild Scottish mist that rattled the doors and lashed at the diamond panes, Julie awoke to gray skies with remnants of dark cloud scuttling along, like black sheep whipped from behind. Full daylight brought slashes of brilliant blue that rapidly broadened until only a few straggling, fleecy clouds rolled by like gamboling lambs. Julie's heart lifted.

She had been informed that Mrs. Mackay breakfasted in bed, and when Moira appeared to light her fire, Julie begged to do the same. Shortly Moira returned with a tray loaded with silver-covered dishes of such savory aroma Julie's mouth promptly watered. Springing from bed, she cried, "Oh, may I have it on the terrace?"

"Surely, Mrs. Boland. But it is a mite brisk and cold out there. Though it is dry enough."

Julie saw no problem with that. The thought of coffee, hot and steaming, with a fine view of the "wee lochen" was more than she could resist. At home she had tramped the beaches in colder weather than this. As Moira carried the tray out of doors, Julie made short shrift of her morning washup, and forced a hairbrush through her obstreperous curls. Then she wrapped herself cozily in a robe of garnet velvet that fell in long, svelte lines to the floor—except where it lazied over the gentle rise of her bosom, and hugged the curve of her hips.

"Ooh, you look fresh as a rose, Mrs. Boland," Moira said on her way out.

"Thank you, and thanks for the breakfast tray," Julie responded.

"Ooh, aye," the housekeeper called from the door. "And you'll not be alone. I just fetched Mr. Ian's tray out there airlier."

Julie went to stone. Beyond the doors her breakfast waited. And Ian with it. Nothing would convince him she had not planned it this way. It was too much. She could not, would not give him that satisfaction, not after last night, and the cutting things he had hurled at her.

She considered waiting until he had finished, but she could see the steam drifting from the center holes in the silver lids, and the aroma of English sausages and eggs was too much. Besides, what if he stayed out there all morning? With a sound of annoyance, she walked straight on out to the sunny terrace.

He did not look up. He was reading *The Scotsman* and dawdling over coffee, the back of his wheelchair, she noticed with relief, walling them effectively away from each other. It was no different, then, from eating in a restaurant. No one *said* she had to address him.

She slipped into her seat noiselessly. Its back was scarcely a yard from his own. Her hand shook as she lifted her juice glass and drained it in a single draft. It was something she never did under normal circumstances, but he had already ruined her leisurely breakfast and she was eager to be done with it. She reached for one of the covered dishes, sniffing its delectable aroma, and lifted its lid with a finger inserted at its center hole. She drew in her breath with a sharp gasp and the thing fell to the stone floor with a metallic clatter.

"I *know* you are here," rumbled a voice from behind *The Scotsman*. "You needn't go to all that silly fuss."

"It was *hot!*" she wailed. "Why do you associate yourself with everything that happens?"

"Very well, now, listen. Breakfast is one meal that I prefer quiet. *Ve-rr-y.*" As he spoke, he circled his chair about slowly. She sprang to her feet as soon as they came face-to-face, reached for her tray, and started back indoors, ignoring the laughter in his eyes. And that other thing, that was not laughter.

"You look very lovely in that color. I like it, Julie."

She did not even pause to answer, but kicked the doors shut viciously behind her.

She had barely settled down to eat at a small gateleg table when without knocking, he opened her doors and rolled himself in beside her.

"I am apologizing," he said. "Won't you pat my head and invite me to join you?"

"No. Is that plain?"

He shrugged. "I've finished eating anyway. I had kippers. Do you have kippers?"

"Ian. I really want to enjoy my breakfast, preferably alone. And then I intend to go riding. And we can both stay out of each other's way until my business here is finished."

"I meant that about your dressing gown. Not only the color. The fit. It leaves nothing to the imagination. I like it, especially when you move."

She set her fork down with a thump. Her eyes lifted from her scrambled eggs. "Do you know something? I liked you better when you were stationary."

"In bed, eh? Aye, it had its advantages," he acknowledged thoughtfully, then added some news. "But I won't be stationary again for long. The doctor was in early. He'll be changing my cast to a light splint and I shall be on crutches awhile. He tells me it is coming along fine. It was only a simple crack of the tibia, apparently, no thanks to you, lass."

"I didn't wish it on you, Ian," she reminded him. "I've expressed my regrets before. And considering what started the whole thing, you had it coming. However, all that aside, I'm glad, and relieved, whether you care to believe it or not. And I suppose you'll be back at your croft, then, in a matter of days."

His eyes glanced off her own. "Well, aye, I'd like that, of course," he said. "But I mustn't rush things, the doctor says. I don't want to be undoing the healing of it. No point in that. I'll still be around awhile. I wasn't saying I'm a well man yet."

She bounced a look off his face, then went back to her breakfast. Without glancing up, she said, "Yesterday you were screaming your head off about going back, with all your retinue over there to look after you, the young girls and all—"

"Aye," he said. "That was yesterday."

She remembered it later on the piny forest trail astride Mairi Mackay's gentle bay. That was yesterday, was it? She knew very well why he looked at her as he did when he said it. She even knew what he thought he could expect when the heavy cast was exchanged for a lightweight splint, and the wheelchair for crutches.

She was not putting the full blame on him. She had made herself wide open for what he imagined lay just around the corner for him. She had, in all candor, asked for it. She had kissed him and allowed herself to be kissed like a woman craving the ultimate. For a few dizzying moments, had he not been encumbered, she might have been swept over the brink—and have found it impossible to explain to herself later.

It was no light matter. True, she was free of any commitment to her marriage; that had died the very instant she had hurled the glass paperweight after Gary. It was dead as a mummified corpse awaiting, in due time, only its legal burial.

But Ian Fraser was not free, much as he liked to believe he could do anything he pleased, when he pleased, with a woman and get by with it on his looks.

Reflecting, Julie wondered idly about Mairi Mackay and her feelings about her grandson's unorthodox behavior. She had not forgotten her vaguely defined remark at their dinner that night at the hotel, about Ian having plenty of time to think things through now. Certainly Mrs. Mackay was not proud of his action, and for all her importance in the glen, she must be very aware that it reflected no glory on the family name. Julie sensed there was also some significance to her insistence that Ian must convalesce at Glenshiel—under her eyes and her influence.

True, it was difficult to assess her attitude toward Audrey from that one time Julie had seen them together, and from her too open expressions about the girl "upsetting" Ian so. But conceivably, even if she were not wild about the girl, that would not very likely matter to a woman like Mairi Mackay once Ian had made his public commitment to her. Honor mattered. And as Ian had phrased it, getting the wedding back on the rails again. These things mattered more than her personal feelings toward Audrey, whose life she would very likely dominate anyway, once the commitment was consummated.

Also, and finally, as Julie saw it, Mairi Mackay clearly held all the best cards. There was no doubt she dearly loved her grandson. But there was also no doubt that he would toe her line or lose his inheritance from her—and for all Ian's bluster, this was a thing he apparently could ill afford.

So, like it or not, he was not anywhere near as free of his obligation to Audrey as he wanted her to believe.

Yet even if she believed it . . .

Once was enough to give her heart to a man, only to have it neatly plucked out and chucked aside. Once was once too often.

Not, of course, that she was so far gone on Ian Fraser yet, or ever expected to be. Oh, she might remember him, but once she left the glen, and the farther away she got from it, the less that memory would mean. True, he had his ways about him—enough to send her riding alone through this lovely forest, rather than linger with him overlong. Knowing she would not trust him any more than—than she would trust herself.

The little bay lifted her head and flicked her ears forward. And almost in the same moment Julie saw through the trees up ahead a tall white horse approaching. In the same glance she recognized Audrey Grant. And despite herself, as both girls' eyes met, Julie acknowledged a shockwave of guilt.

The girl seemed so wholesome in her thick white turtle-neck and riding pants, her pale long hair loose and tossed by the wind. By contrast Julie's image of herself in Ian's arms the previous night seemed soiled and unworthy. She almost wished they had not met.

Yet Audrey seemed in no way cool to her, and almost relaxed compared to their first encounter in Mairi Mackay's presence.

She smiled at Julie, a touch of sadness in her eyes, and inquired how she was enjoying her stay.

"Oh, it's been very pleasant, thank you," Julie answered. "And it's lovely to be riding here. This is a beautiful land."

"I know," Audrey said, that same sad quality in her tone. "I would not wish to leave it, ever."

Julie wondered, had she been contemplating running away from all the humiliation Ian had heaped on her.

"But that should never be necessary," she said kindly.

Audrey shrugged and looked off through the trees. After a moment, as if the matter needed no elaboration, "I really don't intend to. I'm sure this is a passing...aberration of Ian's. He's a bit flighty. Needs to settle down. Father always thought so."

As she spoke, she slipped from the horse and landed lightly on her feet. Julie, sensing the girl really wanted someone to air her feelings to, followed her example.

Minutes later they settled together on slabs of rock in a sheltered clearing she had led Julie to, while their horses followed into the small dell where they nibbled contentedly on some lush grasses. Julie commented on the prettiness of the place, and Audrey nodded. "Ian and I came here so often. It was our place, our little world." Her smile was meaningful.

Julie, not knowing what was expected, murmured, "It *is* a little bit of heaven, isn't it?"

"Oh, yes, it surely is," Audrey answered with a far-off look. "Well, maybe it will be again. After we're married," she said. "I've told Ian I want to celebrate every anniversary here," the last with a girlish laugh.

Julie shot her a penetrating look. "I'm glad you haven't given up on him," she said.

"No," Audrey answered with quiet firmness. "I shan't give up. True, he has caused me a great deal of grief. But I don't think he likes what he's done. He won't even talk about it. He won't give me a reason. Which can only mean there *is* no reason, and he's quite ashamed by now. But when that wears off, I know he'll want to be married after all. Oh, we'll no doubt dash down to England, or somewhere in the south, to do it. Without fuss and fanfare."

"I do hope so, if you still want it, Audrey," Julie ventured.

"I do. I want it badly."

"You love him."

"I adore him. I always cared for him, even before he and his parents went to Australia where his father had just inherited his family's ranch. Ian stayed a couple of years, but then he missed Scotland, and the Highlands. And when he came back to stay at Glenshiel, we—just fell in love. He said I was the most beautiful thing he'd ever seen, and I was simply mad for him." Her eyes shone, telling it, and Julie empathized with her more than ever. To have found such a love, and then to have lost it.

"Oh, I'm still mad for him," she added. "Nothing's changed. Oh, I mean, we've had our disagreements. That croft up there, it really disturbs me. I've wanted him to be sensible and give it up—"

"The croft?"

"Yes. Father says he'll lose his shirt on that. And I'm afraid he will. He knows nothing of crofting, Father says. And he keeps pouring money into it, Mairi's money, which is after all part of our—uh, his inheritance. And as Father says, he'll use it all up before she ever passes on."

Julie felt a sudden discomfort with the direction these confidences were taking; all that talk of money and inheritance. But then, inheritance was very big in this country, and as Audrey had just mentioned, even Ian's father had inherited a ranch in Australia, which was his living. Audrey's father might understandably be concerned for her future welfare; she was his daughter, after all. "I see," she said uncertainly.

"Father worries that there'll be nothing left for us at some future time, except the big old house, and taxes will eat that up some day. I mean Mairi Mackay is a very wealthy woman, but not what she used to be. Father says she's probably using the croft for a tax shelter. But pouring money into it...Oh, well, it's too much for my little brain," she laughed. "I worry more about Ian and the rumors."

Julie cast her a baffled look and found Audrey's eyes steady on hers. "Silly rumors," Audrey added. "And I don't intend to believe them. Oh, I know Ian has had lots of girls before we were engaged. But he's so attractive. Isn't he?" Julie nodded. "I mean, don't *you* think so?"

Julie looked at her squarely again. "Why, yes. I suppose he is."

Audrey seemed to wait, before returning to her musings. "People say—well, people will say anything—but people have noticed all those girls up there."

"Girls? At the croft?"

She nodded. "You see, there's this man who works for Ian. Sandy MacAlistair is his name, and he has several daughters and as you can imagine, they come and go at will in his cottage, supposedly performing various tasks for him. But they happen to be very attractive, and don't imagine for a minute their daddy or mum is going to stop them. That would be a feather in their caps, indeed, if one of them managed to—uh, snare Ian."

"But he's engaged to you."

"Of course. That's what I tell people when they hint and whisper. I don't believe any of it, Mrs. Boland. I just don't." But still, Julie noted, she broke off and dashed a tear from her eye. "It's envy. So many girls wanted him. I never accused him. I told him I didn't believe any of it. Then they began spreading rumors about *me*. Nasty little insinuations, all lies, about me and a cousin of Ian's—just because I was seen in his company. And why not? We're practically one family now.

"Oh, but Ian was consumed with jealousy. He raged at

me. I thought he would strike me. Yes, really. He's a very
jealous man. I'm afraid we had a terrible fracas. But we
made it up, at least I thought we had. And then, well, you
know what happened."

Her voice fell to a whisper. But after a moment, when
it resumed, Julie thought she detected a faint edge. "You
see, Mrs. Boland, if I were the jealous sort, like Ian, I
suppose I'd have had terrible thoughts about *you*."

"Me? But I'm only at Glenshiel on business. I'll be
leaving perhaps this evening, tomorrow at the latest." Julie,
listening to her staccato denial, stopped abruptly, wondering
why such an unreasonable display of guilt?

"Well, that's what I gathered," Audrey said, "but you
understand. I mean, your *being* there, your room right next
to his, and the terrace, and the dressing gown—and Ian
simply refusing to tell me anything." Her voice ended in
a thin wail, her nerves clearly near to a breaking point.

Julie spoke low and rapidly, hoping to cast some oil on
her troubled waters. "Now, Audrey, I had nothing to do
with the rooms. I didn't even know Ian was to be there.
That silly dressing gown—I went through his door from the
terrace by mistake, soaked from a cloudburst, and he tossed
it to me to wear back to my own room. And that's all there
was to it." (And, Julie, you are lying technically as fast as
you can talk, she castigated herself in misery.)

Stemming her tears, Audrey sniffed like a little girl, and
Julie had an urge to hug her for comfort. But then Audrey
was talking again as if Julie had said nothing.

"You were at the hospital. I did see you, Mrs. Boland.
And you managed to get there before me. I had no idea who
you were or what you were doing there. Everything was so
confused, then somebody said later that you'd been with
him at the time of the accident, and before that. That you'd
flown across from the States to be with him."

Julie groaned, hearing her own twisted tale to the police
as she'd tried to cover for Ian, coming back to haunt her
now.

"Oh, my heavens, Audrey," she said. "Everything got
so distorted. The only thing that's true is that we were

speeding him back to the church, for your wedding. And that is all there is, and all there ever was to that story. It's wrong to accuse Ian of things that never happened, you know. The truth, as I see it, is that he got cold feet and yes—wanted to cancel out. But in the end I gave him a good sisterly talk and changed his mind about it. But there was never anything more than that between Ian and me." She grasped Audrey's hand here in an earnest show of candor, while marveling to herself that she could sweep aside those fiery moments with Ian that were pure, unadorned passion—a raw man-and-woman thing—and what good could come of detailing all that for Audrey now?

"I'm amazed," she finished lamely, toying with the bracken at her feet. For Audrey's wide green eyes with their tear-wet lashes were more than she wanted to cope with. Besides, her own part in the thing was over. She was stepping aside, out and away. It would be theirs to patch up as best they could.

She kissed Audrey's cheek when they parted. "I wish you luck," she said and meant it. Then all the way back to Glenshiel the things she wanted to say to Ian burned hot on her tongue. She had gotten a wholly new insight into the man and his activities. Those women at his croft, and all those others that he boasted of, along with all the detailed effects of his lovemaking on them—enough! Oh yes, Ian had a way with him, and except for his cracked tibia (and thank the lord for that) as well as his cracked rib, which he would no doubt have overlooked on her behalf, she might very well have succumbed herself. She'd been that much of a fool!

But no more. She was not about to join that long string of his conquests that stretched, for all she knew, from Scotland to Austrialia and back.

The moment she turned Heather into the stable path, she felt him watching her from the broad terrace that fronted the house. The day being what it was, more sun than cloud, he sat screened behind dark lenses, protected from the wind by a heavy black turtleneck sweater beneath the same tweed

Norfolk jacket he had worn when she met him. It brought
that day back with a quick little tug that was utterly pointless,
considering how she felt at the moment. She hadn't known
him then.

All the way to the stable she could feel his eyes on her
back behind those dark lenses, lingering even as she dis-
mounted and thanked the bay with sugar lumps from her
pocket and rubbed its velvet nose and handed it over to Alec
the stable hand. It was a distance, but she felt that stare of
his burning still when she paused to smile at a lad whom
she instantly knew, from the eager sweetness of his face
and the set of his eyes, was a mongoloid, and doubtless that
young Ben Farquhar whom Mairi Mackay mentioned had
brought that confused message from the lady at Balnain.
She shook his hand and his face split in a warm grin. "I'm
Julie," she told him. "And what is your name?" Alec started
to answer for him, but she held up her hand to let the boy
speak. It came with great effort, "I—I—I am—B-Ben—"

"Well, how do you do, Ben?" Julie said. "I'm glad to
know you." She had known one such, a neighbor's child
in the States, and understood the heartbreaking trials parents
underwent to bring these sweet-natured offspring forward.
Alec seemed bent on explaining. "He's a good lad, he is.
And he does little tasks around here. Comes by on his
bicycle."

"How nice," she said, "You ride a bicycle." She was
aware of addressing him like a child, but he was easily
fifteen or sixteen.

"I—I ride my b-bicy-cle—all over." His arms swept out
demonstrating, and Alec added, "He does, too. Aye, he's
a fine lad."

"I—take letters—and m-messages to people."

Alec winked, and Julie nodded. It was good that they
gave the boy a chance to participate. And he was surely not
the most extreme of such children. She kissed his cheek,
and he beamed. "I'm glad we've met, Ben."

Then turning, she walked swiftly to the house, knowing
Ian's eyes were fixed on her, that she had to pass him to
enter, and even if she knew of some other entrance, she

would not give him the satisfaction of dodging around him. He must not imagine that she was going to come unstrung at sight of him.

She reached the stone walk and moved along it rapidly. When it became unavoidable, she nodded and said, "Hello." She wished he would remove those black lenses so she could tell what he was thinking; and in the next second reminded herself that she could not care less.

He said, "You've been gone long. You're only in time for tea."

She continued toward the door, calling, "That's nice. I'm hungry enough for it." Then with a streak of the devil, added, "I had a lovely day. Met a nice person."

She glanced back saying it, and caught the twist of his mouth. "Did you now?" he said. "And which of our local lads pleased you so, Mrs. Boland?" His voice was rife with sarcasm.

She turned then, laughter rising to her throat. She could not believe it, but Audrey was right. He was a very jealous man. Yet, toward *her*?

She answered softly, "That would be something for *Mr.* Boland to worry about, don't you think?"

"*If* he cared," Ian shot back ungallantly, but she had asked for it.

She covered herself by ignoring it, and smiled a shade too sweetly. "Just so you don't worry about it all night, that 'lad' happened to be Audrey Grant."

And that shook him. She could easily tell.

"And did you have a lovely time of it, disemboweling me?" he inquired.

She hesitated. "We were probably a lot easier on you than you deserve, Ian. The girl still adores you. Don't ask me why."

She left him then and went to change from her scarlet sweater and jeans. She spent more than her usual time choosing from her limited collection of blouses and skirts. Then for some inexplicable reason, she dug out from under all the rest the ruffled silk blouse with its tiny pearl buttons. With a narrowing smile she shook out its folds. She found a modest enough skirt to wear with it, of a heathery blue that hugged her slender hips and flared and swung as she walked. Satisfied, she wrapped a matching shawl around her shoulders against the everlasting chill in the huge rooms, and went downstairs for tea.

But though Mairi Mackay waited there behind her elaborate tea service, the three-tiered tray loaded with sandwiches and scones and cakes, Ian did not appear. Neither then, nor after, when she had gone with Mrs. Mackay and returned from the dusty upper chambers where the antique pieces she had waited so patiently to see were stored.

It was a disappointing excursion. The servants had moved a few items into the doubtful light from the panes under the eaves. She saw a charming rosewood commode of the French Boulle tradition, striking enough to consider the costs involved in transport in the light of what Shirley might hope to sell it for. She saw a three-foot circular convex mirror with a heavy gilt frame. She saw a pair of whatnots and a Canterbury with partitions for music books. And many more. However, these were all nineteenth-century pieces, and not especially extraordinary. "But the table, Mrs. Mackay," Julie had prodded.

"Oh, the table, yes, of course, Mrs. Boland. I'm afraid that is still further back there among those crated items and trunks and all. The men will come to it, perhaps tomorrow. They had so many other duties. I'm so sorry to delay you, but—"

"Well, I suppose one more day won't matter too much."

"Oh, I hope not," her hostess said earnestly. "And is your room comfortable? Does it suit you in every way, Mrs. Boland?"

It was and it did, Julie said, transfixed by Mairi Mackay's black stare. Everything was fine and uh—no, she saw no reason to change. It was indeed a lovely room, and a fine view...

And when she returned to it shortly, he was in it.

CHAPTER NINE

"What are you doing here, Ian?"

"I thought you might not mind telling me," he rumbled from the depths of his chair, "why you went seeking out the little witch?"

"*Answer me, Ian.*" The blue eyes flared, then darkened smokily. Her lips trembled.

"You first, lass. Why did you go looking for her?"

"You're being absurd, and you must know it. I don't even know where she lives."

"Just the other side of the mountain."

"Who cares? She came riding through the forest the same as I. It was purely by chance."

He hesitated, as if assessing the validity of her words. "All right, lass, I grant she rides there a lot."

Her mouth curled, the smoky eyes brightening again.

"You both did, didn't you? To a certain pretty place?"

His face darkened instantly. She thought she had never seen him look hard before, as he did now.

"Aye, we both know the place too well," he muttered.

"You started this, Ian."

"And so I did," he conceded. "But I want you to understand I won't put up with you getting your heads together, you and Audrey, plotting and scheming to bring her back into my life."

She groaned aloud. "I'm very tired of this crazy conversation, Ian. If you don't mind, please go so I can change my clothes."

"Change. I'll go when you've answered me, even if I have to wait around long enough to undo your buttons again."

"At which you're a man of accomplishment, I'm sure."

"The witch has been spreading tales again. And you've feasted on them, both of you and chewed them to bits and had a fine time doing it."

"Oh, shut up, Ian, you're not even amusing."

"I didn't come to amuse you, Julie. Only to set things straight."

"I don't want to hear it, Ian. *I'm tired of you.*"

Her eyes had narrowed dangerously. In a moment she would whirl his chair around and shove him bodily onto the terrace. She tensed, then closed the distance between them in four swift steps. Reaching behind him for the handle of his chair, her wrist was abruptly imprisoned in the taut circle of his fingers.

"You won't be rid of me so easily, Julie." Seated, his eyes were too near her own. It was a mistake; she should have kept her distance. She could not mask the turbulence rising within her, sending blood-hot rivers through her veins. It was there, the excitement he engendered. She knew it showed, in the high warm color of her cheeks, her inability to meet his stare, and the tremor that seized her body, that he must surely feel with his fingers on her pulse. She loathed her lack of control, but she could not conceal it, and his look acknowledged it.

"Answer me, what lying tales has she been pouring into your ears, Julie?"

"No more than I already suspected, Ian."

"About the girls, no doubt."

"You know. Why do you ask?"

"Not for myself," he said. "But I'll not have her besmirching the lassies up at the croft, as she's been doing lately."

"Well! How gracious of you!" Julie scoffed, her head thrown back, observing him through slitted smoldering eyes. "How very gallant, to trouble protecting the young ladies' reputations—*after the fact*!"

"Julie, I do not like the sound of that," he said.

"Who cares what you like!" she snapped with a sudden sharp twist of her wrist that brought only a wincing pain, and not her freedom. "Oh, let me go," she gasped. Then with a burst of muffled sobs as the last of her composure crumbled, "Ian, what are you doing to me?"

For he had tugged ever so lightly and she had fallen against him, and his mouth was hovering above hers.

"Nothing, lass, that you won't have me do, or you'd scream for everyone to hear and not be whispering your protests. Oh, Julie, it is not me you're fighting. It is yourself, and you know that well."

His voice came to her hardly more than a murmur. Then his lips closed on hers hard, stilling her sobs. For a moment of exquisite pain, they bore down bruising and merciless until her body went limp in his arms.

He released her. "Away with you, lass," he said with a soft laugh. "And don't you be listening to lies and half-truths about me."

She came to her feet, feeling exposed, all her barriers searched out and destroyed. Shame was no part of it; only a gnawing certainty that she had painted herself into a corner and that now she was frantic for escape.

She lifted her hands to her face, rubbing her temples. "There were no half-truths, Ian," she murmured. "You are everything Audrey said."

"More than likely," he said. "A womanizer and all that.

Responsible for half the illegitimate kids in the glen."

"She didn't say that. Don't go putting words in her mouth."

"Isn't she putting women in my bed? Including you, no doubt?"

Still rubbing her temples, she stared at him. "You know something? You disgust me, Ian," she said.

"Och, well, it's something. But she will yet, I promise. Likely, though, *after the fact*." The last with that same quirky smile that made her want to strike him.

"There'll be no 'fact,' Ian. The longer you talk, the more you confirm everything Audrey said of you. You'd never make it to my bed, Fraser. There've been too many in yours already."

"What's a healthy man to do?" he countered, his eyes teasing. "And the croft is so handy. To say nothing of the dell in the forest." He broke off suddenly, then resumed, his eyes taking on a glitter she found alien in him, "Oh, hasn't she told you about the dell?"

Her dark brows lifted quizzically. Then her eyes became azure slits. She spoke warily. "You mean that pretty place we sat in?"

"Aye, pretty and peaceful. And the trees tell no tales," he answered, scorn backing his words.

Her mind sprinted ahead to the logical script. She was beginning to get the drift. He was very touchy about that dell. She said, "Hmm, can it be that Audrey, piqued by all your 'womanizing' as you call it, decided to pay you back a bit in kind, Ian? A natural enough reaction, wouldn't you say?"

She spoke slowly, feeling her way, but he did not comment when she paused. He kept his eyes on her, gray as a northern sky, and cold, and hard. "And though she would have forgiven you *your* fun and games, it was not in the cards for you to forgive her, and put the whole thing behind you, and go forward with the wedding. Was it something like that?"

A sudden sense of outrage seized her, a need to champion this, and all women's causes. "Are you telling me, in this day and age, a girl may not slip even once, Ian? While a man can slide down the whole mountain and still come up clean?"

His hands started drumming the armrests. When he spoke, his lips moved stiffly. "I have pledged not to talk of it, Julie. A gentleman does not break a pledge."

Her lips fell open. He was unbelievable. An anachronism. And a paradoxical one at that; speaking from a culture that no longer existed, and a virtuous stand he had no right to assume.

"Interesting," she said, then handed him the truth as she saw it.

"But that same gentleman, Ian, who made a pledge and will not talk of it, will use it quite handily for an excuse to ditch a girl—at the altar!"

She watched the muscles working in his cheeks and saw his lips go thinner.

"That is ruthless, Ian," she added, whispering it in her revulsion. "Low-down ruthless!"

A silence descended between them, so impenetrable the room seemed to darken with it.

Suddenly he spun himself about and propelled his chair toward the terrace. Reaching the doors, he waited only long enough to mutter, without a backward look, "Ruthless is a two-way street, Julie. Someday, perhaps, I may speak to you of 'ruthless.'"

She drew in her breath, seeing him rolling through the doors. Then she called to him, with a sudden, inexplicable ache, "I won't be here to listen, Ian." And again, "*I won't be here.*" She caught his voice riding back to her confidently across the soughing wind, "I think you'll be here, Julie Boland. Aye, you will. And there'll be nobody chaining you to the bed, either, lass."

When she heard the sound of his own doors shutting, she pressed her hands to her heart, pounding so fiercely she could scarcely breathe. He's crazy, she thought. Typical egocentric. And for all his defense of the "lassies at his croft," in virtually the same breath he'd gloried in his reputation.

"And I am supposed to be next in line? Ha!"

Yet . . . her throat tightened. A thin little whimper escaped. Why did she always lean to men who could hurt her so? Why to him, especially? She searched her heart for a long blistering moment, and knew. Because he had this magic about him that roused her hunger, and her crying needs, making them more urgent than any need to be wary of him.

Some men were that way, while others had to work at it. Ian Fraser did not have to work at it. He was loose and easy with it. He knew and enjoyed what he did to women. And because of it, he attracted them to him as moths to a candle. If she were young and inexperienced, she'd be fluttering all over him, like Audrey, trying to reach him, waiting for his arms to open to her again. But Julie had lived enough to know the heat of the flame—and that it scorches, then shrivels, then kills. And she would not hang around here for that.

She turned her back on the door through which he had gone, then paused, riveted to the spot where she had stood beside his chair. She felt her wrist again, rubbing at the tender flesh he had gripped. It still pained, and she lingered there recalling the feel of it with a certain mad fascination.

Suddenly, with a half-choked sob, she ran and flung herself across the bed, burying her burning cheeks in the velvet throw.

When the dinner gong sounded, she did not respond. Later, pleading a headache, she declined a tray that Moira would have brought to her. There was no headache, but there was too much agitation for appetite.

It was time to run. Not two or three days hence, but tomorrow. Early. Even if there had never been an Audrey, Julie could recognize disaster when she met it face-to-face. And Ian was it. He was the epitome of everything she least needed at this stage of her life. All sex, and no substance.

Mairi Mackay's thirteenth-century table, if it ever came to light, would have to sit there. She would not be put off again. She would tell Mairi in the morning.

In the morning, rubbing the sleep from her eyes, Julie stared at the envelope that had been delivered with her breakfast tray, her name prominent on its face. She had never seen Mairi's handwriting, but anything as firm and determined as that had to be hers.

She fortified herself with several sips of coffee before she opened and read it, After reading it, she swallowed the rest of the coffee fast, and dived into her garnet robe. The morning was biting cold, but in her dash along the terrace she scarcely noticed. She knocked, but did not wait for an answer. She did not even care if he were still asleep.

He was not. He looked up from *The Scotsman* with only mild surprise, as if he had expected her.

"What does she mean by this?" Julie demanded. "I mean, if she had only asked—but she's *telling* me!"

He looked her over leisurely, without moving. On a tray before him the steam rose from his scrambled eggs and broiled kidneys. But he seemd in no rush for those either. He returned her look as if she were some oddity he'd found under a rock.

"Ian!"

"I haven't the faintest idea what you are talking about, lass."

"Well here, read it. It came with my breakfast."

"Aye." He took Mairi's letter from her and read, nodding with an occasional, "Aye," and "Hmm, gone to Edinburgh, Richard driving her. Ooh, aye, old Uncle Hugh is acting up again." He threw her a grin. "He's eighty-two but he still bears watching."

"All right, Ian. I got all that. Mrs. Mackay left last night to attend to whatever emergency your 'old Uncle Hugh' has got himself into. She'll be gone several days, perhaps longer. But the rest—"

"What rest, lass? Why don't you settle down? Here, sit here." His hand patted the edge of his bed.

"No way. Listen, Ian, I can well understand a family emergency. But what on earth made Mrs. Mackay appoint me your—custodian?"

"Oh, did she now?" He smiled, and her hands curled until she felt the nails bite into her palms.

"Oh, did she now," she mimicked, baring a white and

wicked smile. "You *see* what she wrote! Would I be so good as to keep you occupied so that you don't take some idea in your head about sneaking up to your croft! Ian! What exactly does your grandmother consider keeping you occupied?" She caught the sly lift of his brows and gave him no chance to answer. "What makes her think I would care to stop you, anyway, if that's where you wish to go? On the contrary, I'll help you pack!" Then, at a sudden thought, "Why on earth doesn't she want you back at your croft? You're not dying."

"Oh, I daresay that's to keep me away from all the lassies up there," he responded promptly, winking, and she glared at him, assessing his look to see if he was laughing at her, or about his grandmother. But his eyes fell again to the letter.

"Aye, and you're to see to it that Audrey doesn't upset me, as Gran puts it, because I need my rest."

"Bunk! If she comes by, I shall personally deliver her to your room. But why has she loaded all this on me, Ian? I've got to get away from here."

"Why?"

"Because I've *got* to. I don't have to give you reasons."

"Aye, but that's my Gran. You remember I said as much. She'll take your life over, like everybody else's."

"Not mine, Ian," she responded with a toss of her head that set her sleep-tangled curls dancing. "*I* am leaving. After breakfast. I'm sure there's someone about who can drive me to the train?"

"No doubt," he said without a moment's hesitation. His eyes lingered on his grandmother's note.

"Whom shall I ask?"

He looked up at length as if he'd forgotten she was there.

"Oh, yes, you want to leave. Well, tell Moira to ask Alec to bring the van around. He'll take you wherever you want."

"Oh. Th-thank you," she said, and waited, not knowing why.

"If that's what you want, Julie."

She carried his look back with her—cool, penetrating,

it had seemed—and the sound of his last words, almost a question, as she bucked the wind on the terrace. She sat with it, and ate her chilled breakfast, and wondered if she would be leaving so abruptly had it not been for Mairi Mackay's manner in *telling* her what she wished done, rather than asking, or even suggesting.

It came to her that it is not a very courteous thing she was doing, running off when her hostess had a serious problem elsewhere, and thought well enough of her to rely on her in her absence.

Nevertheless she was packing her bags when Ian thrust himself through her door. She did not look up. She felt the winy flush spread across her cheeks and dared not risk his seeing. She remarked only, when he remained silent, "Perhaps the van can drop you at your croft, too, on the way."

"You've asked Moira about Alec?"

"No. I was just about to."

"I'll decide about the croft, when you've asked Moira."

She knew what he was saying; if she left, he would leave. If she did not . . .

Her head swam. She felt adrift in a sea of vacillation.

"You won't be leaving, Julie," he murmured suddenly, and with such assuredness, she turned on him in alarm.

"Ian, I don't want to get involved with you. Haven't I made that clear? You're a games player—with women. You're playing with *me*."

"But you're holding the cards, lass," he said softly. "You can finish packing those bags and leave, and well you know it. Or you can stop—get involved or no, as you wish, I'll never force your hand. It'll be your own choice. And that you know, too."

Heather flicked her ruddy ears and responded eagerly to Julie's hand on the rein, turning her head homeward.

"All right, back to your nice dry stall," Julie said. It was a dreadful day for riding. Alec had probably thought her mad, but there had been hours before train time, and for herself, the damp, chill winds were far preferable to the crackling fires on Glenshiel's hearths.

Earlier Ian had left her abruptly, wheeling himself out, not waiting for her response. As if all that needed saying had been wrapped up in his final taunting challenge.

Taunt and challenge it had been, too, its echoes filling the room when he'd left, ricocheting from wall to wall until the clamor was too much. She had not found Moira, but had gone directly to the stable where Alec said, "Aye, mum, if it's the seven twenty-eight you're wantin', I'll bring the van around at six. But there's an airlier one, also, mum, for Edinburgh. Before five, I believe."

"N-no," Julie had told him, turning it over in her mind. "Thank you, Alec, I'll be ready." She made no mention of Ian moving up to his croft. It was not her concern, and she had no plan to see him before she left, other than to call a hasty good-bye on her way down.

As she rode from the stable astride the doughty little bay, she was absolutely determined on her course. Hunched against the showery gusts, her snowy turtleneck protected by a shell the color of the native rowan berries, she knew she was doing what had to be done. Too vividly she remembered the ease with which she had let herself be charmed by Gary Boland's lean, lithe body, and the loose lazy way he moved. As if that was all there was to love, and marriage, and *life*.

To say nothing of another woman's prior claim on that charmer back there.

Julie had hoped before she turned the horse homeward again to have the luck to run into Audrey once more to say good-bye. And possibly in so doing, to dispel any lingering doubts the girl might have about herself.

It was nearly four thirty when the bay lifted its sugar lumps daintily from Julie's palm, and she tramped the distance to the stone terrace, assuring herself all she needed was a cup of hot tea to brace her, and she would be on her way with nary a look back.

A small chill rippled along her spine, but it was solely of the weather. Her jeans were black with wetness where rivulets of water had streamed from her rain gear. Her dark curls were darker and curlier still, tangled by fingers of wind, and her lashes so laden with drops she had to blink to see.

One thing she saw was a silver Porsche standing in the great curving drive, and as she passed it, she looked ahead to the stone terrace and blinked again. Several times. Whatever it was standing there, framed in the open door, she saw through a shimmer of color and light.

She did not break her stride because it was not a thing that concerned her. Moira was there, too, and as Julie dashed the water from her lashes, she could see the housekeeper's upturned face aglow with a kind of worship. Yet it was not Moira's face that brought her to a sudden halt at the foot of the steps.

Nor was it that she had never before encountered men in kilt. She had seen—and already concluded with a sense of revelation that the kilt was more masculine (and sexy) by far than what she was accustomed to seeing on men— be it tight jeans or three-piece suits. But this was something else.

Whoever he was, with his blue-black hair and hawkish nose, and his heavy-lidded hazel eyes that grazed her only briefly—courteously, she sensed—he was born to the garment as animals are born to their skin, birds to their feather.

Tall—taller than Ian whom she had never seen in clan attire—with shoulders broad and square and graced by a dark blue jacket that contrasted smartly with the kilt's lively green and red and gold tartan, he might have stepped straight out of legend. He *was* legend, Julie thought. Surely men like that no longer walked the earth.

He was conversing with Moira. But for one magic instant as she found her legs and climbed the steps and went to pass within feet of him, something of him reached out and touched her. He did not stop his train of words. He did not fully look her way. But she knew when she came within the range of his glance. She felt the brush of it on her cheek, resting there a flickering moment, like a tongue of flame.

Her knees went weak as water as she walked into the house. She did not hesitate, or look back, but floated trance-like to the stairwell and took the steps one by one to the floor above, sufficiently dazed that Ian's presence in her room once again swam only vaguely to her notice.

She said, "Hello," in a small wavering voice. Then, the breath rushing from her throat in a long drawn sigh, she added, "I have just seen—*a vision!*"

CHAPTER TEN

"YOU HAVE JUST seen," he said after a ghastly silence, "*the baronet*. Aye, Duncan MacKinnon. In the flesh. And if I had a pound for every lass who has looked at him as you look now—and promptly raced to his bed—I should be as rich as he is!"

The beatific glow drained instantly from Julie's eyes.

"And hopefully as courteous too?" she lashed at him.

"With holdings all through the realm."

"And a little less gross, perhaps?"

"Even a castle in Northumberland."

"And—oh, my cup runneth over—maybe less bilious with envy?"

They broke off sharply and together. It was as if the space they shared was too tight to contain their mutual contempt.

Julie was the first to resume, measuring him with open distaste. "I have never witnessed a more blatant example of petty, spoiled, rotten-kid jealousy." The last hanging on her quivering lips, there came a sudden recall. Her eyes went wide. "He's—he's your cousin, isn't he, Ian? Oh, no, of course you're not about to like *him* again, after—"

"Say it, Julie. Let us get that much straight!" He was glowering beneath his thick drawn brows, daring her, she thought.

"You know what I'm referring to," she answered defiantly. Her hands fell to her hips, her head shot up. Blue fire leaped from her eyes. He would not dare pursue it, she thought. But—

"Aye, I'll say it for you. You mean after Audrey crawled to him in her pretty little dell, eh?"

She flushed, and he seemed deliberately to stretch out the moment, taking pleasure in her embarrassment, before adding to it.

"Aye, but that is not the reason she is not my wife now, nor ever will be. And that is as much as you need to know, Julie Boland. That, and that I had no stomach for Duncan MacKinnon when we were children, nor have I had any since. And as for any apologies that he came to deliver, he may stuff them. Along with his condescending ways about my croft and the life I choose to lead. And so, if it is your 'vision' you wish to see again, it won't be in my company, Julie."

That much she lobbed straight back at him. "I said nothing about seeing him again."

"Only because you've had no time to think of it." He began propelling himself toward the doors, but lingered to add, "I wouldn't be putting it off, if I were you. He came north for the grouse in August and stayed for the stalking. But there are warm beds waiting on him in the south. The man is *busy*, lass. And you wouldn't want to miss out."

"Get out of here!" she breathed. "Again you disgust me!"

He wheeled his chair about and met her stare, hard. "It was the stars in your eyes, speaking for you, lass," he said, expelling each word with a disgust to match her own. "And

I've seen it before when the MacKinnon sweeps this glen, and well I know the signs. But—ooh, aye, I forgot," he added as if it had just come to him. "You'll be leaving Glenshiel. And what a pity. To be missing out on all that."

Julie reeled. It was as if he had set her up, a live target, to torment with arrow after poisoned arrow; the last, and most enraging, implying that if only she were in the neighborhood, she too would follow every girl to the baronet's bed—she, who had never yet exchanged a word with the man! Abruptly she knew what Audrey had meant about Ian's insane jealousy.

But his gall was so monumental, it could not go unanswered. Moreover, what Ian failed to realize was that he had just hurled down a gauntlet, and there was no way that Julie Boland would fail to pick it up!

When her breath had steadied, she spoke in a voice that sounded alien to her ears. "I hope you hang around for the fun, Ian. Because I am not leaving after all. No. I shall stay on just as long as your exciting baronet is here at the glen. And I will very happily keep you informed on his progress."

She could make nothing of his expression after that. It seemed as static as a photograph. No line, no muscle moved. She thought, good! That shut him up. But when he wheeled himself about again and left without a word, she felt cheated.

She was not surprised when she saw Moira carrying his dinner tray to him. He was going to mope and sulk; it was his style when crossed. When the housekeeper smiled at her, remarking, "Mr. Ian is not himself this evening," she barely refrained from responding, "You mean there are times when he's actually pleasant?"

Instead she told Moira, "No use setting the dining table for me alone. I'll gladly take a tray, too, if you don't mind."

And so she did, and though it was lonely in her room, and distracting with the muted sounds from beyond the wall, it was surely better than the sort of company Ian could have offered.

Later, carrying her after-dinner Grand Marnier with her, she descended to Mairi Mackay's well-stacked library where she settled down with a book before a lively fire on the hearth. She was deep into the volume on clan history when she heard Moira walk swiftly through the main hall to answer a peremptory knock at the door.

"Oh, good evening, sir," Julie heard her exclaim, breathless again, and knew at once it was Duncan MacKinnon. But this time, after a muffled exchange, Julie caught the placating doubt in Moira's tone. "Ooh, I shall see aboot it, sir. I shall go straight up and ask Mr. Ian. I cannot say if he will have company tonight. He was not at his best."

Her ascent up the stairs came to Julie labored, and reluctant, but it was Duncan's patient pacing in the foyer that held her attention. She thought it was rather decent of him to return, knowing what the bullheaded moose's answer would likely be. Seconds later it became patently obvious as Ian's roar thundered down from above.

"I damn well will not see him and you can tell him I said so, and if he cares to come around after the healing's done, I'll give it to him in more than words."

Julie came to her feet, appalled. It was not her affair, but her reaction was to spring to MacKinnon's defense at once. Ian's attack was outrageous, devoid of any show of manners or decency, landing her at once in MacKinnon's camp. She felt supportive of him, and though she had never been introduced, she had a strong desire to express her indignation on his behalf.

With Moira descending the stairs again, she edged toward the door until she could see MacKinnon waiting, his face lifted to the housekeeper, an air of patience about him, as if he felt sorry for the woman and would spare her having to deliver such a painful message. Her admiration for the man soared when he lifted a gentling hand, waiving away Moira's need to go on. Julie thought, Duncan MacKinnon is of a different breed, a different world, and Ian Fraser could not even set one of his big feet through that door. She liked the way he held Moira's hands in his own, commiserating with her a moment. Then it was that the housekeeper's glance leaped to her across the room and MacKinnon, turning, saw her.

After that Moira withdrew, making no effort to see him to the door, perhaps because she sensed in some way that if she chose in that moment even to swing from the great crystal chandelier above them, neither of them would have noticed.

He came to Julie slowly where she stood in the library entrance, pausing when he stood a short distance off to bow ever so slightly. She smiled and nodded, remaining wordless. Just as she had thought moments before that Ian was not of MacKinnon's world, she felt herself, too, a little alien to it. Once again it flickered through her mind that MacKinnon was the stuff of legends.

Handsome in a dark way, a mysterious way, she had the sensation of studying him through the frame of a portrait. When his smile deepened and his black eyes narrowed as if savoring what he looked upon, seconds passed before she realized it was herself he was concentrating on; and then only after he reached his hands out to her, palms up, inviting her own. Not unlike what she had just observed his doing for Moira Eddington. But not like, either. There was an indefinable difference, and that difference brought a quickening at her pulses.

She was conscious instantly of the garment she wore, a caftan of a gossamer silk, turquoise in color, though lined with peach satin that shimmered through with a tantalizing contrast. This she had packed with her for those relaxed evenings when she knew she would dine alone. Now, though MacKinnon's eye never for an instant left her face—unlike that other person's, wandering disgracefully at will and forming judgments along the way—Julie knew he had missed nothing. The soft folds that descended all in a piece from the tall ruffled neckline to the floor left everything beneath to the viewer's imagination. MacKinnon's imagination, she felt reasonably sure, was not busying itself all over her body. She felt no sense of wariness as she laid her hands in his, and murmured, "I'm Mrs. Boland, Mrs. Mackay's houseguest."

"I am *delighted* to meet you," he said so emphatically it brought a rush of warmth to her cheeks. He still held her hands. It was as if he had forgotten, and though she gave them the merest tug, nothing happened. She allowed them to lie there then, enclosed in his warm smooth palms. It was curious that she made the contrast in that moment, recalling Ian's which were hard, and calloused—and rough, too. As rough as his manners, she thought, smiling up at Duncan MacKinnon again.

"I don't know why I should be apologizing for Ian's atrocious manners, S-sir Dunc—uh, your l-lordship—" She reddened fiercely, uncertain what one called a man of his rank. He laughed aloud, his head flung back and his dazzling white teeth contrasting strikingly with his almost blue-black hair and tanned complexion.

"Try 'Duncan,' my dear," he told her. "Only that, if I may call you—?"

"Julie," she offered at once.

Then they were laughing together and Julie was telling him how silly she felt, but such things were unknown where she came from.

"America, of course," he said. "Your speech, and—other delightful differences."

They had moved into the library and sat together now before the fire to which he had thoughtfully added a log. He knew his way around Glenshiel, naturally, Julie noted. He found a liquor cabinet and refilled her Grand Marnier. Then searching out a brandy glass, he poured himself a measure and joined her on the sofa where once again she spoke of Ian's behavior.

"Ah, but that is Ian being Ian, my dear," Duncan dismissed it with a soft laugh. "We in the family are accustomed to him. We don't take him too seriously. Ian's problem, of course, is that dear Mairi dotes on him entirely too much, and is inclined to forgive him things she would never forgive in others, such as—well, the recent wedding fiasco in which I seem to have been snared up, quite without reason."

"Oh?"

"Candidly, Julie," he added, "it is why I've been trying to see Ian. I really want to set this thing straight and correct a few notions he's formed about me and...Miss Grant before I leave for the south. Ah, fill your glass, my dear?"

"Oh, no," Julie declined, smiling. "I've had too much as it is." Her head was indeed spinning; but it had hardly anything to do with the cordials. The man was a charmer, and she could well understand why Ian wanted to put him down. Also, why it disturbed him so to think that Audrey might—or might not have, who knows?—gotten ever so close with Duncan MacKinnon who was all too likely to be a marvelous lover...and a very hard act for Ian to follow.

MacKinnon was leaning toward the crackling flames, reaching for a cigarette from a gold case. His hawklike profile edged in the firelight was breathtaking. Yes, Ian had reason to worry.

He turned suddenly, catching her eyes on him. She looked away uncomfortably, but knew he'd seen. "Cigarette?" he offered. She declined, avoiding his hooded gaze. If he was aware of having an effect on her, he gave no sign. Yet he stirred her in a curious way; it was something about his mouth, the shadow of a smile, one-sided though it was, as he held the cigarette between his lips and searched out a gold lighter from the sporran at his side. His movements were sure, and graceful. Julie's eyes, following, traveled to the spread of his kilt, touching down a moment on his muscular calves in their thick white hose, banded by garters of forest green. She felt, rather than saw, his eyes trailing hers, and looking up quickly, flushed with guilt. He did not laugh, as she expected. Rather he flicked his lighter, and in the sudden hot flare as it touched his cigarette, he shot at her a look that pierced the last of her reserve.

In that single glance she knew she could never have matched his own. Reserve was what Duncan MacKinnon was made of. Whatever emotions he managed to shield with it, she might never know. Nor, she knew intuitively, did she wish to explore. Enough to keep her own in check and not wave them like banners snapping in the wind—in the way she'd been brandishing them at Ian. But then the two men were so different. And this one was utterly intriguing.

It pleased her, but did not surprise her, when he asked her to dine with him the following evening. By the time he rose to leave, they had shared a pleasant hour in which Julie had learned more of Scottish history—its clans, its regiments, its wars—than it had ever entered her head to inquire about. Duncan was a superb storyteller. The time fled by, the images he drew stalking across her mind like sets in a great theater. Smiling down at her at length from his great height, he reached again for her hands and lifted Julie to her feet.

She felt strangely exhilarated. The evening had been unlike any she ever remembered. She found him knowledgeable on such a variety of matters there was no way she could compete. And not once, never, had the conversation gone personal. Not even in extending his invitation.

"May I count on dining with you tomorrow evening," it was. And she had answered promptly, "I should love that, Duncan."

He would call for her about eight. She walked with him to the door and waved as he stepped into the silver Porsche. When she turned back, her eyes were glowing. She saw that in the tall pier glass at the top of the stairs. She held her cheeks between her palms and gazed back at her image, a trifle incredulous. She was honest enough to acknowledge that she came close to being beautiful in that moment.

And honest enough to wish that Ian could see her now.

CHAPTER ELEVEN

DUNCAN MACKINNON WAS a magnificent host, she learned to no surprise the following evening. The dinner, a masterpiece of culinary craft, ordered in advance of their arrival at the inn in what seemed remote wilderness to Julie, was served in a private, candle-lighted cubicle reminiscent of nineteenth-century clandestine affairs. Julie found it deliciously amusing, though this was neither an affair, nor any way clandestine, and Duncan's behavior was so unfailingly correct she wondered if he was aware of the paradox. As late into the courses as the poached salmon, caught only that morning in adjoining waters, Duncan had yet to top the compliment his eyes had paid her when she descended the stairs at Glenshiel to greet him.

That look, the sudden flash of fire beneath his black brows, had said it all.

But then she had seen to it. And not solely because it was exciting to dress in the one formal gown she had packed, a striking affair of pale cream silk that shaded to pink and then, where its wide circular hem swept the floor, to the deepest ruby. The neckline, if such it could be called, eluded one tanned shoulder entirely, while barely securing itself to the other with a rose—plucked, as it happened, from the long-stemmed beauties that Duncan had ordered delivered to her that afternoon. She had received them with breathless pleasure, and pinned the largest of them to her shoulder moments before he was due at Glenshiel.

It was a gesture that pleased him, she knew from his face; from his eyes, especially, that reflected a healthy masculine appreciation. "Charming, my dear," he said as she had hoped he would.

But that was not the reason she had elected to dress as she did, and to top it all off with his rose. She had been driven, rather, by the devilish hope that there might come a confrontation with Ian before she left. Certainly he was aware of her impending date with Duncan. Moira's delight on hearing about it when she delivered Julie's breakfast tray must have resounded all the way to Aberdeen. Julie was not quite sure why she wanted Ian to be aware. Spite was a fair guess, but she would not own up to that. He had it coming, was all she acknowledged, savoring the situation.

When she'd stepped from her room to the lighted hall, she knew his door was ajar for she felt the draft at her back. His lights were out, or very low; she did not trouble to see. But Moira, bless her, was just then carrying his dinner tray to him and paused to gasp, "Ooh, Mrs. Boland, you look every bit a princess tonight."

"Thank you, Moira," Julie laughed, tossing carelessly after her, "I'm sure I shall have a royal time!"

Whether he glimpsed them from his window shortly after as Duncan helped her into his car, she could only speculate. It was of small consequence. The blow had been delivered, and right on target.

Meanwhile Julie was finding herself much more relaxed with Duncan MacKinnon than on their earlier meeting, and somewhat less in awe. There was no need, she quickly discovered, to be on guard with him, as was always the case with Ian.

Once again Duncan displayed that erudite brilliance that had kept her spellbound the night before. He had journeyed, it seemed, to the ends of the earth. Places familiar to him at firsthand were known to Julie only from magazine articles and travel brochures. He spoke with authority on India, where in the mid-1800's his family had fled the Sepoy Rebellion. He spoke of the aftermath, and the many changes in the course of the years. He spoke of South Africa and his grandfather's regiment in the Boer War. His wide grasp of people and places and history held her in thrall, and except for those moments here and there when he paused, unexpectedly, and his gaze seemed suddenly to rivet on her upturned face, her lips moist and parted in the shimmering candlelight, her eyes shining with admiration, no word that could be construed as personal passed between them. Not, that is, until they were on their liqueurs, and then what happened rather startled her.

With no special lead-in, Duncan asked, "You are married, Julie?"

The question had been tossed at her so abruptly it took seconds before she could fit it in the proper slot. A scant moment earlier he had been telling of the Forty-five, Scotland's tragedy. Now this. She nodded, a trifle uncertain.

"Yes," she said at length. And, composure returning, "That's over now." For it was, and she saw no reason to explore it further with Duncan. She even felt a shade of irritation with him for bringing it up at all. And yet since she had introduced herself as *Mrs.* Boland, a man had a right to know if he was entertaining an actively married woman. Perhaps what troubled her vaguely was that he seemed to have asked it with his eyes as well as his lips, and somehow it had encroached on the easy relationship they had established together.

Nor did it help when he added, flashing his white smile again, "I've always found married women—far more interesting."

At that, Julie stiffened. A coldness spread over her that he could not possibly miss.

Long after, tying events together, Julie wondered if this was the moment when Duncan MacKinnon had unwittingly placed them on opposite sides of a barrier; a low barrier, to be sure, across which they found much entertainment in each other. But beyond which she, for her part, had little desire to poke about.

For the present, however, the incident was a soon forgotten intrusion on the richness of the evening. By midnight, when Duncan saw her to the door at Glenshiel, making no effort to enter with her, she felt easy enough again to agree to a drive the following afternoon. She even felt a touch of guilt for having frozen up so visibly at a rather commonplace question. And really she might have acted a trifle more sophisticated about his subsequent comment on married women, and its less than subtle implications. It was just possible that Duncan had little panache with innuendo.

There was no repeat of the scene the following day. He chose the route to the beach at Nairn where they walked briskly for a time along the rocky shore of the Moray Firth, the damp, chill winds twirling Julie's hair into a mass of shining ringlets. Droplets hung from her lashes, and her smooth skin glowed. But when she shivered from the cold in spite of the thick Icelandic sweater she wore, and Duncan's arm shot around her shoulders seeking to warm her, she managed soon enough to disengage herself—without making a thing of it. Or so she thought.

He did not touch her again, except to guide her among the larger boulders. Nor did he seem to resent what was clearly a signal warding off too much physical contact between them. He reacted with deference.

They picnicked from a hamperful of delicacies he had brought, ranging from caviar to fine French wine, and Julie returned to Glenshiel pleasantly weary—and curious about what Ian was thinking. She had seen nothing of him for two days. She had only heard the sounds beyond the wall, and now, long after crawling between the satin sheets, sleep was hard to come by.

There were those feelings she was trying to define, about Duncan for one thing. She had never known a man like him, and beyond a doubt, he was the most intriguing she ever hoped to meet. Even his maleness ran like a dark undercurrent in him, where in other men, Ian, it was flaunted like flags at the head of regiments! Much, much too obvious.

Added to Duncan's subtlety, one could hardly deny his abundant good looks and the way he carried them. The gray tweeds and stalker's cap he'd worn this day were every bit as exciting on his tall loose frame as the colorful kilt in which he usually appeared. What the element was that was lacking in Duncan was what baffled her now. She could not pin it down. She knew only that while she enjoyed his company enormously, she was always willing to say good night to him, always a little worried that he might ask her to kiss him. On this last occasion she had even been inclined to beg off another date for the following evening. She had accepted only for want of a logical excuse. He *knew* she was alone, and unoccupied; that Ian was as good as not even there! How could she pretend? So it would be dinner again tomorrow night and the theater at Inverness.

Julie's days began to blend into a pattern; rising, exclaiming at breakfast over the flowers that arrived each morning, Duncan's standing order from an Inverness florist; then preparing for that day's, or evening's date, fully enjoying it, and finally returning to the room a wall away from Ian.

Finally she had not seen him for six days. She counted back once lying in bed, acknowledging of course that there was nothing lost, after all. What woman dating a man like Duncan MacKinnon could complain because Ian Fraser preferred to sulk in his room?

Although when Julie probed her mind thoughtfully from time to time, she had to admit to a little trouble with Duncan's utter correctness. No, of course, she did not want him to relax his courtesy to her. She would feel uncomfortable with his arm around her, and she was grateful more than he'd ever know that he had never tried to kiss her, because it might have ended right there. Nonetheless she rather missed something that had been hers and Ian's; while they had raked each other savagely, she had had no problem relating to him. She could tell Ian anything, and obviously he held nothing back from her, no matter how irksome. She would never dream of telling Duncan anything personal about herself, or her past. Perhaps he would welcome it. Perhaps it would bring them closer. (Too close?) Or... perhaps it would not, because he was after all a gentleman born and bred, and she of a different world. She accepted, even cherished his flowers and his pleasant companionship, without craving more. And it was this combination, the flowers and his charming behavior that led to a clash with Ian which just fell short of violence.

This time, however, Mairi Mackay was the catalyst.

As it happened, it was Mrs. Mackay's second phone call from Edinburgh; the first placed a couple of days earlier had begged Julie's forgiveness for being so long absent. There was much turmoil in her brother's affairs and her stabilizing influence was needed there. Meanwhile she hoped that Ian was providing sufficient entertainment during her absence.

Julie answered that all was very well indeed, and she would stay on until her hostess returned. Ian, she supposed, was well enough, although she had not seen him lately. However, she was having a ball.

"I've been seeing quite a bit of Duncan MacKinnon, Mrs. Mackay."

Julie was fully aware of Mrs. Mackay's too lengthy pause that ended at last with one word, "Re-al-ly!"

Nor, assessing it, was there anything about that "really" to reflect Ian's nasty appraisal of the man, despite the fact that the British can pack an awful lot into that word.

There *was* a note of surprise. But then Mairi had no idea that Julie had even met the man. If she had asked, Julie would have been quick to assure her that Duncan was treating her like a queen, and had done so from the first hour in his company.

But Mrs. Mackay had drawn back and asked nothing— then. Which may have led, Julie could not help speculating, to the second call a couple of days later. This time Julie could feel the velvet-gloved interrogation about affairs at Glenshiel. She was never afterward certain how Duncan's name plopped into the conversation this time, but there it was.

"No, Mrs. Mackay, Ian still refuses to see Duncan."

"And you've not been able to persuade him, Mrs. Boland?"

It startled her. "I haven't tried," she answered. "Was I expected to?"

Mrs. Mackay hesitated, but for no more than a second. "Well, I know Duncan has business in the south, my dear, and I'm sure he's eager to get away. It is apparently a matter of conscience with him, however—over something or other he feels he has to apologize to Ian about." Julie turned that over in her mind, but would not be drawn in on *that* little matter. "I know he would want to leave there *friends* with Ian, if only my grandson would agree to see him. That would resolve it, I'm certain, and poor Duncan can be on his way."

"I believe," Julie said after a moment's rapid thinking, "that Ian would listen to you sooner than to me, Mrs. Mackay." She did not trouble to add that Duncan seemed in no hurry to leave for the south or anywhere else. That, in fact, she was taking a long drive with him that very afternoon. It was nothing she wanted to discuss with Mairi Mackay whom she was beginning, rather dimly, to read like a book—a book in French, perhaps, of which she had only a faltering knowledge.

"Ian," Mairi resumed after a thoughtful pause, "will not only not listen to me, he will not take my calls, dear."

At that Julie's thinking underwent a reluctant turnabout. Privately she thought his action ill-mannered and disrespectful, but was not altogether sure of what she could do about it.

"I'll see him, Mrs. Mackay," she promised. "At least, I'll try."

"Thank you so very much, Mrs. Boland," her hostess concluded only to add, on the point of hanging up, "By the way, has Audrey been to visit?" And when Julie assured her she had not, Mrs. Mackay murmured, "Perhaps it is as well. I'm afraid they could hardly be civil to each other now."

Julie hung up once again with the feeling of "reading" Mairi Mackay, falteringly; and as with a foreign tongue, seeing certain words come through clearly, and certain others filled with shadings of meaning totally beyond her.

Was it possible, for instance, that Mrs. Mackay was not as eager as Julie had believed for an eventual culmination of Ian's marriage to Audrey? Could it be that she was not moved by tongues wagging in the glen? Had it really been necessary for her to advise the girl not to push her luck with him by seeing him too frequently?

It seemed preposterous, and yet, each time she had phoned, and each time Julie had hung up, it was with a vague sense of having been skillfully probed, even manipulated. So skillfully that Julie was only now beginning to wonder about Mairi Mackay's sudden trip to Edinburgh. Such a long way from Glenshiel. And Ian and herself. In that great mansion, alone.

Which was the laugh of the year, Julie thought, considering all she and Ian ever wanted was to claw each other to death!

She had seen nothing of Ian for a week. He had not closeted himself like a recluse, but he had made very sure that their paths never crossed. For her part Julie cooperated to the nth degree, making her goings and comings audible enough that there was no chance of their accidentally colliding in the upper passageways. Similarly she was alert to the clatter and hum of the lift, and refrained from showing herself until he was well out of range.

He was in his room when she hung up the phone on Mairi Mackay. He was always in his room in the mornings. The mornings were the worst—something about his nearness, a wall away, when she wanted to be thinking of other things. As what to wear when next she saw Duncan. Or this or that thing he had said, or look he had given her...

Yesterday the doctor and his youthful assistant had called and she had longed to ask Moira later what had happened. But it was embarrassing since Moira could not but be aware of their feud. Better leave it so.

Yet now, after Mairi Mackay's call, the sounds from Ian's room leaped at her with disturbing intensity.

She did not go at once to see him as she had promised. It had been easier said than done. She delayed, resolving in her mind what to say, and how to say it, so that he understood she was merely delivering a message from his grandmother to whom he refused to talk. But when suddenly there came a series of puzzling thumping sounds from his room, nearing his door to the hall, on an impulse she dashed there to meet him.

Her sketchily rehearsed greeting—"Ian, I have a message from Mrs. Mackay"—never passed her lips. He was *standing* in his open door, and he was propped on crutches. Their stares welded, until she stammered, "I—I'm glad you've progressed. Oh, I see they've changed the splint. How nice, it'll be easier." And a foolish stream of things she could not seem to stem.

He said, "Thank you." And after a strained silence, "You wanted to see me? Uh, come in."

Awkward on his new supports, he moved back and she passed into his room and waited until he came up behind her. Her glance brushed a suitcase lying open and half-packed on a luggage rack. But it made little impact in this untenable moment. He swung himself around finally until he faced her and she started mouthing the little practiced speech.

"Ian, your grandmother has asked me to—to urge you— to make up this foolish quarrel with—"

"The MacKinnon," he cut her off so scathingly she flinched. "My grandmother grows more meddlesome with age. And as for the baronet, I have no liking for him, but neither have I a quarrel. He managed to open my eyes once. And—" his look suddenly lashing her like a whip—"from all appearances, he may yet again!"

Her head snapped up as if he had struck her. "I don't

know what that is supposed to mean," she challenged.

"A bright young woman like you, Julie? Need I spell it out?"

"S-spell it!" she dared him.

"All right, then. You like him, lass? This collector of women like trophies? You, too, hungering after his bait—his estates, his castle, his wealth, *and* his title? '*Lady MacKinnon*'! Now that must make music in your ears. As it has to others, Audrey among them, and all of them not hesitating to offer their wares for prior consideration—"

He broke off, catching Julie's wrist with ease a bare inch from his jaw. She was white with rage, and so too was he.

"No, you'll not slap this away so easily, lass. I know him—and his women, too, the grasping, social-climbing lot of them."

"*You're a liar*, Ian," she cried, struggling to be free. His crutch was no deterrent; his hand did not give. It hardened, but the pain went unnoticed. "I've dated him, and I will again and again—"

"It's what I said."

"And not for any of the things you're implying. Duncan is being maligned, and by jealous, envious people like you. I should know. To me, he's been everything a woman wants. He's never laid a hand on me and he's a joy to be with: knowledgeable, charming, and courtly."

"*And rich*, say it, damn it! You'll be crawling to bed yet with your knowledgeable, charming, courtly gentleman—same as all those before you. Same as Audrey Grant herself."

"How long, for heaven's sake, are you going to hammer away at that tired, worn-out old excuse for running out on your own wedding?"

He released her so abruptly that she fell a step backward. She watched as he hobbled to his open suitcase, where rummaging a moment, he brought forth a rumpled envelope from which he whipped a pale pink badly creased piece of notepaper. She caught a whiff of fading perfume as he held it aloft. Approaching her, he muttered, "As long as the ink can be read on this paper. This. *Here!*" He thrust it before ier, but she backed off. "Written you will see on the morning of the wedding. And delivered to me at dawn. *To me*, Julie, at my croft. By young Ben Farquhar who had brought all her sugary notes to me there before, when *I* was courting her. And how was the lad to know, he couldn't read. And if she'd told him a dozen times to carry it where she wanted it to go—to Duncan MacKinnon at his chalet—the poor lad wouldn't remember, or know whose name was upon it. But you'll know. Look for yourself."

She shook her head, dismayed, not wanting.

"*Read it!*" he roared.

She started to turn, to run to the door. He blocked her way, with a crutch, and then with his body. She covered her eyes. "I don't want to, Ian." But he seized her shoulders, digging his trembling fingers into her flesh until she cried out in pain and the tears bit her lids.

"It's no matter to me what you want," he said hoarsely. "Nor what you do with Duncan. If that's your taste. Matters only that you do not leave the glen believing Ian Fraser a liar! Now read this and you can go. *I have no wish any more to hold you.*"

He thrust it at her and she had no choice. The fragrance swam again to her nostrils. The girlish scrawl danced before her eyes.

> My darling Duncan, If you love me as you said, there is still time. Send me word before eleven, when I must leave for the church, and I am forever your . . . Audrey.

Julie's stunned gaze crept to him. It was as if an earthquake had devoured the ground beneath her. His smile was the iciest she had ever seen. "Aye," he muttered, "and hearing nothing from her lover with his title and his fortune, why then, the lass came to the church to be the wife of the crofter instead. Having lost the grand salmon, she casts her line again for the littler fish! You have called me callous, and ruthless, Mrs. Boland. Have you a name then for Miss Audrey Grant?"

There was an urgent need to answer, but nothing came from the logjam of crippled defenses massed in her head. She wanted at least to say she was sorry for having misjudged him. And she wanted not to have to talk of Audrey. The thing was beyond all comprehension. She wanted most of all to say what she needed without mentioning Duncan. For it was impossible that this man who had accorded her such respect and deference could have been in any way responsible for Audrey's calculating maneuver. But before she could sort it out, Ian was at his door, opening it and standing beside it leaning on his crutches; waiting with elaborate patience for her to remove herself. To pass by him, and go. When she lingered, he said, "I'm sorry, but I must go and ask Alec for a lift in the van."

Then it was that her glance dropped again to the suitcase; this time meaningfully. "You're—?" Her eyes widened.

"Going home," he said. "To the croft."

"Oh—" The foundations beneath her seemed to rock ominously and threatened to crumble away.

She moved to him, her eyes forward, knowing that his were withdrawn from her, making no effort to see. When at last they stood together in his open door, she paused.

"You're—really going?" she murmured, the quiver in her voice beyond control.

He nodded. She saw that he would not be drawn into discussion. She saw that she had receded from his thoughts, from any importance in his mind. She had become incidental. She realized for the first time that until now she had been very aware of his interest, expecting it; then taking it for granted. Their mutual rages notwithstanding, she had come to count on it. It had filled a void in her life, in her heart, with something very solid, very real. And now it was leaving her, slipping away with the seconds, while he waited for her to go.

She stepped past him into the hall. When she spoke, she did not turn, or try to recapture his eyes. She said, "Won't I see you again?" Her voice came thinly, almost strangled.

It took him forever to answer, as if he were turning it over in his mind whether to answer at all. When she was about to move on, he spoke. "I will not go looking for you, lass. You'll have to come to me—and take your chances."

She felt herself sinking, reaching out in panic for something to grasp, finding no handhold, not the frailest straw. Then touching bottom, suddenly she rose again, caught in a dizzying surge of revolt. He could not write his own rules and expect her to abide by them. Hurt, misunderstood though he'd been, the dictum he handed her still smacked of jealousy. And she was not quite healed of the poisoned darts he'd slung at her with such abandon, and still not taken back a word.

Did he really imagine she would ever go looking for him at his croft? Forget it, Ian Fraser, it'll be a long, hot day in January.

"Then I'll say good-bye now," she told him stiffly, and walking rapidly to her room caught his careless retort.

"Whatever you say, Mrs. Boland." And the thud, thud, thud of his crutches carrying him to the lift.

CHAPTER TWELVE

THAT AFTERNOON, IN the early Scottish twilight, Duncan kissed her for the first time.

Reviewing it later, Julie thought, Maybe it would have all felt different if he hadn't done it *that* afternoon.

He had called for her only a short while after the van, with Ian in it, had rumbled away, and almost before she had finished dressing for the drive. The silence beyond the wall had reached to her like tentacles, then abruptly withdrew at Moira's usual breathless announcement at her door.

"It's the baronet, Mrs. Boland."

Julie had to smile. Some day Moira was going to faint announcing Duncan.

She had gone to greet him, and seen him rise from the sofa where he had waited, his hand outstretched for hers. It crossed her mind that he was not at all as Ian painted him. If

she thought he were—a man who would deliberately set
out to have a brief affair with his cousin's fiancée—she
would have quit seeing him on the spot. But wasn't there
ample evidence that Audrey had been the instigator? And
a man pursued by something like that, meeting it face-to-
face in the right place and at the right time, would not be
inclined to back away. Certainly he had made every effort
to apologize to Ian. Ian would do well to swallow his stub-
bornness and shake hands with his cousin and forget the
entire episode—especially considering he had not lost very
much in Audrey Grant.

"You look ravishing, Julie," Duncan said with his flashing white smile.

"Thank you, Duncan," she said, noting how easily he
said it, with none of the sexual overtones that would signal
a girl she'd better be alert for problems. Actually she did
not feel ravishing; she had dressed for the drive perhaps too
carelessly, slim-fitting jeans again topped by the warm Icelandic sweater. She had not been in a mood to fret about
too much casualness. But Duncan, too, had forgone for-
mality and wore rough tweeds with a cashmere turtleneck.
With his black hair tumbled across his brow, Julie had to
admit he was still the most striking of men.

The road he chose to drive bore them north and west
toward the coast, as magnificent and sometimes isolated a
land as Julie had ever encountered. Off the main road, itself
largely a single lane except for laybys, he sent the feisty
Porsche climbing higher and even higher among the gray-
green gorsy braes, their monotony broken only by the random boulder and the sheep, as far as her eye could travel.
Lone sheep, or sheep in grayish clumps, scarcely lifting
their heads from their grazing.

Then at last a hut, with a thin coil of smoke lazing darkly
to the sky. Julie shivered. It seemed impossible that people
lived here, and bore children and reared them...

"You are exceptionally quiet today, Julie," Duncan remarked, when his smile prompted little response.

"Oh, I...I was just wondering how people can bear

such loneliness." Her hand swept the far reaches of the land to the distant mountain peak.

"All they've ever known, I guess," he said mildly. "They're contented enough, I'm sure. Good people. Hardworking. Productive. Except for Scotland's curse—the bottle. Ah yes, that fellow who lives over there"—he nodded toward the hut that had triggered her interest. "When I hired him—"

"You—*you* hired him, Duncan?"

"Oh, certainly. It's part of my land we're driving on."

"Then you're a crofter, too, like Ian?"

He laughed. "No. I own the land. The man's my crofter. He rents from me, and of course, produces. He gets his share and I get mine. As for Ian—Ian's croft is part of his inheritance still to come, and I am afraid my Great-aunt Mairi is much too indulgent with him. But," shaking his head, "Ian seems to believe that a man must use his own hands and break his own back or it is not really his. A pity, because Ian is never going to realize any profit, the way he's going. He has a few lads up there helping him, paying them unheard-of wages, and Ian, very simply, is heading for disaster. He'll lose his inheritance before he ever owns it." Listening, Julie was reminded of Audrey and her fears about Ian's croft.

Suddenly as they drew closer to the crofter's hut, she saw the woman of the place. She was bent over a rusting iron tub in the yard beside a black hole of a doorway, and she was scrubbing clothes. Julie saw it with something akin to shock.

"They—they have no water in there?" she wondered aloud.

"They have a well, and a pump—a hand pump naturally, since there is no electricity."

"But there are lines nearby, Duncan. I saw them."

"Of course, but these people are used to this." And with a low chuckle, "They wouldn't know what to do with electricity if I had it drawn in, which is very costly, as you can imagine."

She assimilated that slowly and murmured at length, "They just might learn." But if Duncan heard, he made no response. He slowed a little to wave to the crofter's wife, and the thickset woman lifted her broad face and waved back, smiling. Then she wiped her brow on her upraised forearm and went back to her tub.

"Shouldn't we have stopped, Duncan?" Julie asked when they had passed. "It's so lonely there, wouldn't she have liked to talk?"

He smiled down at Julie again, she thought a little patronizingly. "She has her work. I would not want to break in on it. She'd very likely stop and make us tea and scones and the usual—"

"And what's wrong with that, if it gives her a break, Duncan?"

He spun the wheel and took a narrower road descending to a valley before he answered. "It's always so close in those houses. I can scarcely breathe. You wouldn't like it. The smell of dampness—"

"But, Duncan, they breathe it all the time," she answered, knowing as she did that he would skirt it. "And what of their children? They grow up with it, don't they?"

"And go off," he said. "To the cities. Sometimes to University—"

"And never come back?"

"Unfortunately," he said. Then after a moment, "Makes it devilishly hard to find help as the old people die off."

She slanted a look at him, wondering if he did not realize that with better conditions, the young would return. And yet, she thought, he was not a hard man. He had not spoken of his crofters with scorn. He had sounded paternal about them; caring, but not interfering—rather as a man who understands the custom of the country, which Julie had to concede she herself did not. The woman had not looked back at him darkly, with hate. She had smiled and waved and gone back to her work as if it was no matter to her that her laird and his lady had the leisure to drive about on a weekday afternoon in his fine silvery Porsche while she must scrub the family wash by hand in water she had pumped-laboriously outside her smoke-blackened hovel.

"Are they all like this?" she asked. "Ian's croft, too?"

"Ian's—well, no. Ian's done some work on his. Expanded the original structure that was in ruins when he took it over. Not bad, the work he's done. Only foolish. He's not likely to occupy it himself after Glenshiel is his; and it is really above a crofter's head to appreciate—" He broke off abruptly, slowing down. "Would you like to see the place? It's not too far away, Julie."

"Ian's croft? Oh—oh, no—no, Duncan. He's there now. I don't want to go." He studied her a moment thoughtfully. Then driving on a few yards, he pulled up into a layby.

Leaning back in his seat, his eyes seemed to search her face for a time. "Ian's gone back, then. Does that bother you so much, Julie?"

She sensed there would be no evasion with Duncan. Besides, she felt him a good friend, no more. No harm in admitting, "We had a bit of a row." Without adding that Duncan himself was at the center of it. "I don't wish to see him again."

"Is that why he left? Your quarrel?"

"No, not at all. He was packed to go when it started."

Duncan remained silent for so long she wished he would take the wheel and drive again. She could not meet his eyes, though she felt them pulling for hers, fixed now on the mist-shrouded horizon.

"You fancy the chap, don't you?" he said all at once, and it crossed her mind that the statement was very uncharacteristic of Duncan; much more personal than he had ever gotten with her.

"He's a friend," she shrugged.

"And you would like him to be more?"

"Duncan! Isn't that a little silly, now?" He unnerved her, but she opted for laughter. "You can like a man and still not want *more*. A girl doesn't hanker after every man who crosses her path."

He smiled. "But for this man you do a little, don't you,

Julie?" He spoke low, almost to himself, his eyes assessing her.

For the first time he began to irritate her. Whether he realized this or not, he started the engine again and they drove more than an hour with the most perfunctory of polite talk on his part, pointing out historic sites, scenes of old clan wars, or places of exquisite beauty for which he had a genuine appreciation.

She quickly lost all sense of direction since he did not always hew to the main road, but they had come down from the barren stretches to the greener, bracken-carpeted braes, and she knew that he was heading homeward again. She felt unaccountably relieved; nothing had changed, and yet everything seemed different, as if the light through which she saw him had dimmed, and his outlines were no longer sharp and clear.

When he stopped on a rise overlooking a spattering of small lochen far below them, she felt a vague tension returning.

"Do you know where you are?" he asked, pointing to a stretch of forest on the far side of the lochen where the land rose steeply again. She shook her head and he explained, "That's the forest you rode through, and up ahead there—where the woods taper off—that is Glenshiel."

"Oh, I see it now. We're on the other side of the glen."

"Yes. You can just barely see the house, but its loch is the last of this chain. You can't see the lodge or the chalets where I stay when I come north; they're beyond the crest. But there, look over there, Julie." He pointed directly before them to where the forest thinned, and where a sudden flash of dying sunlight fell upon a craggy stretch of soil and a dark, bleak, low stone house that hugged it.

"That is Ian's croft," he said abruptly. "Now you see it, and you need not meet him."

Her lips fell open, startled. Her eye grazed the scene and came away, reluctant to display any interest before Duncan. He appeared not to notice, but resumed as if she had inquired.

"Below—it's too dim to see now—are his grain fields. The sheep graze the high pastures at his back. And there are a few cows. And horses. The cottage is stone, of course, and from what I can see, he has added a new slate roof and perhaps a room or two more. But it is still a typical crofter's dwelling."

"Duncan," she interrupted at last, "why are you telling me all this? All those details? Why did you bring me here? I didn't ask—"

He turned to her then, resting one arm on the wheel. "You wanted to know, Julie. That was obvious. And besides, *I* wanted you to know how Ian lives. Because that is the way any woman he marries will live."

"Why tell me?" she reiterated, openly annoyed.

He hesitated. She could almost feel him shaping his response. It came in a question. "Why are you still here, Julie? Mairi has been away for some time, with no certainty about when she will return. If you did not prolong your stay because Ian was at Glenshiel, why then did you? Or—have I the right to hope I had something to do with that?"

Then for the first time he slipped his arm around her shoulders and drew her, stiffening a little, closer. Her reaction was to freeze. Then to lie.

"I feel I should wait until Mrs. Mackay returns. She is my hostess."

His voice came to her softly through the twilight invading the car. "I would feel truly encouraged if I could believe that, Julie. At least that Ian had nothing to do with it." He seemed to wait for affirmation, but she gave back silence. She felt his hand tightening on her shoulder.

With a suddenness that sent a cry from her throat, she was in his arms, his mouth so close to hers she felt the moisture of his breath. Then it broke like a flood.

"Julie, I love you. I loved you from the first sight of you in the rain. And I want you. I have so much to offer you— no barren existence scratching a living out of the soil. I love you, you must believe that, and I want to do things for you that nobody has ever done before. I want to take you all over the world, to places I know, among people worthy of you—worthy of *Lady MacKinnon*. Oh, my dear, Julie, you must listen to me." She was struggling now, futilely, in his unyielding arms. His mouth fought for hers as she tossed her head from side to side, until with a shuddering groan, he captured and held it—and to her everlasting horror roused a meager instant's response in her. It was his maleness demanding of her; her femaleness *betraying* her. But it was only for that scantest of moments. And that was the moment he chose to believe.

Releasing her, he breathed in deeply, audibly. Then he murmured, "I have my answer, Julie. I know how to reach you. Oh, yes. *I know how to reach you . . .*"

CHAPTER THIRTEEN

I KNOW HOW TO REACH YOU.

The words chilled her through the sleepless night, spoken as they were with such evident satisfaction. As if he had discovered in her some *thing*, some quality that stimulated him. A response he liked to find in women. She had fought him, and he had enjoyed it. And now it frightened her, and she hated herself for the moment her own body had betrayed her. But forever fighting a man off was certainly not her idea of love. If Duncan actually thought he was "reaching" her, he had much to learn about Julie Boland.

Even before he returned her to Glenshiel, she knew she would leave on the following day.

He had kissed her good night at the foot of the terrace, and she had let him. She had stood very still and felt his mouth close on hers and made no response, knowing how resistance inflamed him. He had said, "I'll telephone you; we'll have dinner," and she had answered, "Very well," knowing she would not be there to take his call. Then she had gone to her room where, moments later, Moira had brought the message that Mrs. Mackay would arrive the day after next.

She felt locked in. She *had* to wait for Mairi Mackay now. She could not run off, knowing that Mairi had left the message for her, expecting to find her there on her return. But she did not have to be around where Duncan could phone or find her.

Mulling over future moves, she attended to a thing she had meant to for days. She phoned the States and got Shirley on the line and informed her she would be leaving the north and would keep her posted as to her whereabouts. She checked with her on events at home, then sensing a reluctance to speak, amounting almost to secretiveness on Shirley's part, she pressed her for news.

It came quickly, a hissing little whisper into the mouthpiece. "Gary." Julie gasped. "He's there? Now?"

"Right outside the door," Shirley said. "He's been hanging around for days. Lonesome, he says. Hurt because you left. And I suspect nearly broke."

Julie said, "That's what my letter did." Then quickly, "I'll be in touch."

She hung up and drove the nightmare from her mind. There was too much developing here. Gary had made his own lumpy bed. She would not be back to share it.

Presently she was scrambling for some excuse to evade Duncan. By morning she still hadn't found one, other than making herself scarce. And so she mounted Heather and pointed her head to the trail again.

She had told Moira she would be gone all day, and the housekeeper had obligingly provided a lunch for her saddlebag.

"And if the baronet phones?"

"I'm not in, Moira."

The housekeeper looked as if she could not imagine not

being in to Duncan MacKinnon. But she murmured, "Yes, Mrs. Boland."

Julie felt as if a load had fallen from her, at least for the time being. It was a day to enjoy; windy, as the Highlands are always windy, and cold, but with an indigenous kiss of mildness.

Early on, she greeted several pack-carrying hikers climbing the narrower trails to the crest, and a couple of forestry men laboring in the underbrush. But other than those, the only sounds were bird calls and the scurry of startled woodland creatures. From time to time she peered through the trees for glimpses of the opposite rise beyond the chain of lochen, where yesterday Duncan had "mapped" for her the land through which she now rode, with Glenshiel at her back, and miles ahead where the forest sheared away, a dark stone cottage squatting on its rugged terrain. She had a flashing mental image of Ian moving around its dim interior, content at last, having washed her from his mind— in a way she wished with all her heart she could wash him. If she continued on this trail, eventually she must emerge from the forest not far from Ian's croft. Musing on that, she fantasized idly what might happen if she went and casually knocked on his door. She would never actually do it, of course; not after his challenge to her. It was only something she could not dispel from her thoughts, as she knew she would not when she had gone from here... wondering always what might have come of it.

She was enjoying her lunch sometime after, propped against a boulder in a grassy little nook while the mare nibbled close at hand, when the flick of its ears alerted her to company approaching. Almost at once Julie recognized the intruder and would have given much to avoid this second meeting with Audrey Grant. She had so little heart for it now, and at Audrey's expression, she had even less. The girl had not yet seen her, and her classic features seemed rigid with determination, her mouth a thin, tight line, while a small frown puckered her brow. Had she really changed that much, Julie wondered? Or was she seeing her for the first time through new, and clearer eyes.

The sympathy Julie had communicated to the girl on their first meeting was gone, and there was no way she could, or would, dredge up a facsimile.

Then abruptly Audrey was aware of her. Her eyes widened, startled. But she laughed, greeting Julie in a friendly way.

"How nice to see you again, Mrs. Boland."

Julie smiled. "Care for a sandwich? It's quite good."

But Audrey declined. "I've just come from tea, thank you." And after the minutest hesitation, "I was on my way to—uh, has Mrs. Mackay returned yet? I understand she's been away."

"She's expected tomorrow," Julie answered and saw the girl's face relax.

"I see. Well, I'll just ride over and see Ian, then."

She smiled and would have sent the gelding forward, but Julie stopped her. "Wouldn't you have gone if Mrs. Mackay were home, Audrey?"

That the question should have been asked at all seemed to catch the girl off guard. But she answered candidly enough, "I would prefer not, Mrs. Boland."

It shook Julie, that kind of outspoken honesty. The girl seemed unreal. Here, she thought, is the same young woman who planned to run out on her bridegroom in order to marry several rungs higher on the social and economic ladder. And having failed in that endeavor, attempts without a qualm to win back her erstwhile groom. The same girl, Julie suddenly recalled, who resorted to an almost childish ruse of luring Mrs. Mackay away from Glenshiel via a message delivered by young Ben; to send her miles off and out of the way so she could sneak in and see Ian alone—a ploy, Julie realized now, that Mairi Mackay saw through at once. Here, then, was a girl who will stop at little for her own gain. And now, as if her answer required some elaboration, "I'm afraid Mrs. Mackay has felt all along that I am not quite good enough for Ian. It's family, I suppose. Mine is only two generations from the Aberdeen fishing docks. Fishing was their living, Mrs. Boland, and I see no shame in that."

Julie was dumbstruck by the defiance in her tone. "Surely, Audrey, nobody else does, either. Not in this day and age."

Julie saw the angry flare of her nostrils. "I'm sure you can't understand. Perhaps it's different where you come from. But I have felt Mairi's antagonism. It's very real and I am certain if it weren't for her, Ian and I would have patched up our quarrel and been married before now."

Julie hesitated, wondering if she dared inform Audrey where it was that her foolish and highly compromising note to Duncan had wound up on her wedding morning. But abruptly she decided it was not her place to do so. That eventually when Ian got over his rage, he would tell her; but that if she never found out, it might be her just deserts. As for Mairi—

"I think you are wrong about Mairi Mackay, Audrey, at least for her reasons for what you call her antagonism. I am sure it has never entered her head to care about your family's beginnings."

Audrey's chin lifted. "What other reason would she have to put so many stumbling blocks between Ian and me? Haven't I always conducted myself . . . properly?"

Julie searched the girl's face in silence until the moment stretched too long. Then she said, "I don't know, Audrey. Have you?"

She felt an instant chill between them. The girl's hand tightened on the rein; she would have bolted ahead. But again Julie stopped her.

"Ian is not at the house, Audrey. He is at his croft."

Her quick drawn breath was audible to Julie. "Is he?" And when she nodded, "Have you been to see him there?"

"No." Her short answer drew a penetrating look from the girl.

"You were going there, weren't you?" Audrey said.

A buttress of resistance hardened in Julie. She left the

question hanging between them until the girl added, "You do fancy him, don't you?"

Julie rose from the ground and carefully gathered the wrappings from her lunch and stuffed them into her saddlebag before answering, with a question, "Why are you asking me that, Audrey? Why discuss it at all? If you're bent on winning Ian back, why not get on with it? You know where he is. There's nobody standing in your way."

When she spoke, her tone had softened again. "I suppose, Mrs. Boland, I wanted to make very sure that we are not on the same track. Ian probably let himself go with you a bit. The two of you alone in that house, your rooms so close. I mean, I could forgive him that, and you as well."

Julie turned her back, feeling the statement did not deserve a comment. But Audrey added, "I would rather not be enemies, Mrs. Boland. Please believe me. But I *had* to see him alone. I didn't want any—interruption while we're together, Ian and me."

In that spirit Julie was moved to inquire, "Are you sure you're doing the right thing, Audrey? I mean, going after him when he doesn't want to see you?"

The girl sat taller in her saddle, her face suddenly brooding. "If you want something enough, Mrs. Boland," she said, "you go after it. My family would still be in the Aberdeen fish markets if they hadn't lifted their sights above that. I do not apologize for going after Ian. I—love him."

"I see," Julie said, seeing much more than the girl intended. Seeing, for instance, that Audrey's sights, as Ian had broadly hinted, had a way of traveling upward—*randomly*. And that this once they had unfortunately overshot their mark. For having thrown herself at Duncan, who obviously preferred to physically battle a woman for possession of her, she had done herself out of the chance to become Lady MacKinnon.

"I supposed I shall go now," Audrey said. And yet there was still a moment's hesitation. "You've been seeing Duncan lately, haven't you?" she added, and Julie nodded. She could well imagine it was all over the glen.

"I saw him yesterday."

"Yesterday!" The girl's voice was suddenly electric with excitement. "Oh! That must have been before—Oh, you were so lucky not to have been with him when his car rolled over up near the lodge!"

CHAPTER FOURTEEN

JULIE, REPLACING THE bit in Heather's mouth, spun around.

"Oh, my heavens! Was he hurt?"

Audrey seemed to take forever to answer. "Well, somewhat, yes. I don't know how badly."

"He's at Raigmore?" Julie asked with a sinking sense of déjà vu.

"Oh, no, Mrs. Boland. The doctors go to the baronet. He's still up at his chalet at the lodge. I don't know why you haven't heard. The news would have carried."

"I left Glenshiel early," Julie said, already parrying with her conscience. How could she not go and call on him? Until yesterday he had treated her royally. Yesterday might have been a fluke. Besides, he had not carried it further than that kiss. But even so, the man had been injured after seeing her home. Shouldn't she——? "I don't know how to get there," she said lamely. "I shall have to return to the house and perhaps Alec will drive me there."

"Oh, not at all," Audrey told her. "That will take forever. Besides," she explained, they were only now a short distance from the track that veered from the path they were on toward the lodge and the chalets. "I can show you, since we're going the same way."

It was easy enough to find, Julie realized later, though much farther than Audrey had led her to believe. Eventually, however, with the northern twilight tinting the mists lavender, Julie stood before a chalet which a groundskeeper informed her was Duncan's. For the first time a shadow of doubt drifted over her, for the man had looked at her oddly when she inquired if Duncan was able to have visitors. He had answered, uncertainly, "Ooh, I'm sure he doesna mind, mum. He has visitors often." But he did not expand, and hitching Heather to a nearby post, Julie approached the chalet with reluctant steps.

She had barely knocked at the heavy oak door when it swung wide, framing Duncan himself against a warm glow of firelight. Duncan, whole, and standing upright, with not so much as a Band-Aid in sight.

"My *dear* Julie, how good to see you," he exclaimed, his voice reflecting some astonishment. Julie fell back as if a fist had struck her, her first reaction scorn of herself for having allowed herself to be duped, and by a girl whose track record for deception had already reached Olympian proportions. Clearly there had been no accident. Nothing at all had happened to Duncan. By sending her off with this hoax, Audrey was merely assuring herself that Julie would not break in after all on her tête-à-tête with Ian. Flushing with anger, Julie pinned it down at last, recalling Audrey's searching statement about Ian letting himself go with her at Glenshiel, and her *forgiving* him the indiscretion. What she really meant was, "You two may just care for each other nore than I like, and so—" Now, over there at the croft, f Julie's name came up, and Audrey would be certain that t did, she would drop the word ever so casually that she had just encountered Julie on her way to see Duncan at his chalet. Yes, she would do that. And while it should mean little to Julie what Ian thought, it came roaring over her now like a storm off the sea that it meant more than she cared to admit. *It meant everything.*

All in a flash it passed through her head as Duncan's hand reached for hers. Numbly she let it rest in his and stammered what sounded, even to her own ears, an unlikely explanation.

"I was told—that something had happened to you. An accident. Your car turned over." She could hardly believe it herself, telling him, and his slow smile chilled her. "It's true," she added vehemently. "Audrey Grant told me."

The smile thinned a trace. "Ah, yes, the pretty little vixen," he said softly. "But there was no truth to it, not surprisingly. Still, I thank you, Julie. You were concerned enough to come to see me."

He paused to wave to a fellow guest who passed on the piny path joining the the chalets. Julie glanced over her shoulder and noticed others returning, apparently from the day's stalking.

"I'm glad it was a false alarm, Duncan. But I think I had better go. It's getting late. And cold."

"I'll ride with you," he said at once, and it came as an agreeable surprise that he did not invite her into the privacy of his chalet, though the open door revealed the cozy warmth of sheepskin rugs and tartan throws slung casually among the chairs and sofas, all a-shimmer in the light from the blazing hearth.

"If you'll wait a moment, Julie," he said and disappeared only to return with a plaid, in the MacKinnon tartan, she noticed. This he tossed over his shoulder as he rejoined her.

He smiled, his black eyes filled with good humor. "The nights are cold," he said. "I thought you might need it." Was he teasing? She could not be sure.

She nodded, and stood there woodenly grappling with her doubts. Common sense said she'd never find her way down the slope and back to Glenshiel with night in rapid descent. That same good sense inquired, But with him?

Still he had made no move except to hold her hand in greeting. He had not asked her inside, had not offered her a drink from the collection of bottles she'd glimpsed on a sideboard.

How much had she misjudged him, she wondered, this man who, after all their many dates, had finally gotten around to kissing her. Why had she attached so much significance to the manner of that kiss. To his apparent need for a woman's resistance before he could enjoy her. Now here she had come to his presence, and he had not even invited her inside. He had offered to see her home, as a gentleman would, knowing she could never find her way.

Suddenly it was as if he could read her mind. His voice held a note of reproach, if not sadness. "You're standing here with fear in your eyes, Julie. Have I ever wronged you? Or is this a natural feminine reaction when a man kisses a woman and tells her he loves her and wants to marry her?"

She brought her guilt-laden eyes to his. It was true, nothing more than that had ever happened. Then he offered a final thought, heavy with irony.

"What has the—ah, pretty vixen told you? That I—assaulted her, perhaps?"

"Oh, no," Julie gasped.

"Or," he smiled cynically, she thought, "rather that I finally issued orders to keep the girl out of my chalet where she developed an irritating habit of turning up, uninvited, at the most inconvenient times."

"Duncan, please, I don't want to hear all this."

"Though it is true," he added as if she hadn't spoken, "that I slept with her once. But not here. A very unfortunate fall from grace, as it turned out, and I regret any damage it might have caused. Though in the long run, I would say Ian was well served. Now, Julie, I have been honest with you. And if you're still inclined, I'll ride with you to Glenshiel."

Trailing behind him, Julie followed Duncan down the unfamiliar terrain. She was glad she had had the courtesy to apologize to him. He'd brushed it off, his mood on the rise. But she was mostly glad that he was with her, for the way was dark and tangled.

Their conversation had turned to lighthearted trivia until Julie mentioned that Mairi Mackay would return the following day. And that she herself would leave immediately after.

Instantly, as if a pall had settled, she sensed a subtle change. It was not alone Duncan's silence, as if turning over the news. Nor even his half-jesting, half-earnest acknowledgment, "So you will not linger awhile—with me?"

To answer, no, the only truthful answer she could give, was too baldly cutting to the man's ego. She hedged it with kindness. "I have no choice, Duncan. I really must be getting on with business."

The pause that followed, filled only with hoofbeats, stretched painfully between them. He broke it at length.

"That is all you have to say, Julie, to my proposal?"

She answered only with silence, long and drawn out, and then unexpectedly he wheeled his horse and closed the short space between them, halting only when their two mounts stood side by side, their sleek bodies nearly touching on the narrow trail. Duncan's black towered over Heather, just as he towered above Julie.

"What are we stopping for, Duncan?" she protested, her eyes eluding his. "Can't we get back to Glenshiel and talk? It's frightfully cold."

For answer, he drew the wool plaid from his shoulder and started to toss it to her, only to finish by guiding the length of it around her body, his hands lingering at the task until she remarked, "That's quite good enough, Duncan. Can't we go forward?"

"Not yet," he answered evenly, and to her bewilderment she saw him dismount. With a slap at the black's haunch, he sent the beast a short distance off among the trees and turned to Julie with outstretched arms. She felt instant wariness at his approach, but she was not really afraid. Still mounted, she could send Heather into a gallop and be off before he knew. She was not precisely lost, either, even in the near dark. They had reached the main forest track minutes earlier. It was hard packed and fairly well defined with just enough capricious moonlight filtering through that if driven to it, she could find her way home—with Heather's help, the intelligent mare being no stranger here. So her response to Duncan was to ignore his waiting arms and reiterate her desire to proceed.

His hands had dropped to her waist, and from his great height his eyes were only a little beneath hers.

"There's no hurry, is there, Julie? It's not nearly as late as it seems. Come, let me help you down. Let's sit awhile. There is so much I want to say."

She went rigid as his powerful hands tightened at her waist. They were so large she could feel his fingers nearly meeting at her back.

"I'd rather not, Duncan," she said, deploring the tremor in her voice. Deploring, too, that she had not sent Heather into a gallop seconds earlier. Her advantage was lost; he had only to drag her down and let the little mare go her way. She pulled back slowly, carefully, hearing the voice of caution in her head. Don't fight him. It's what excites him most.

Aloud she said with an effort at laughter, "This is quite silly, Duncan. We could have talked at the chalet." Then she stopped, seeing his slow smile.

"I've been honest with you, Julie. I'll be honest again." He scarcely moved his lips saying it. "There were too many about up there. I had a great need to feel alone with you."

Her heart nearly stopped, but she kept her head. She must pretend it was all for laughs. Laughter was her last defense, and she let a trickle of it fall from her lips now.

"You've been watching too much television, Duncan. Honestly, I can't *believe* you." Then, lowering her voice dramatically, *"Really, my deah young lady, I had a great need to be alo-one with you—"* Then she broke into gales of laughter, that ended in a strangled cry of alarm, "No, Duncan, *don't!*"

She felt herself dragged from the saddle, the wool plaid tangling around her legs, restricting every effort to kick herself free. She had enraged him, and now she was terrified.

"I'll not be mocked, Julie," he said. "Never make sport of me." Suddenly it was the voice of a stranger.

Her breath lodged in her throat as he held her to him, his face so close she could read his flaring anger in his eyes, and feel the heat of his mouth near her own. She strained for the ground beneath her, but the wretched plaid, though fallen from her shoulders, would not be dislodged. His arms ringed her like bands of steel. She gasped, feeling his lips burrowing beneath the high collar of her sweater and closing wet on her throat. She writhed in panic. Don't fight, don't fight, memory cautioned. Play it cool . . . But her frenzied mind retorted, Cool, hell! This is no game!

As her balled fists pounded his face, his low laughter sent shafts of ice all through her. Her fists turned to claws, raking his cheeks until he flinched and his head drew back involuntarily. But his laughter persisted, hideously.

Suddenly she was on the ground, her arms widespread, his hands pinning hers to the soil. Terror possessed her, a terror so tangible it sat like a demon on her breast. The man was mad. She was in a wilderness a thousand miles from nowhere with a madman staring down at her and *smiling*. She could not draw her eyes away. Not from his slitted gaze savoring her anguish. Not from the hawkish curve of his nose. Nor his blue-black hair slanting from his brow and brushing her own. Even in the extremity of her plight, it shot through her mind that he was diabolically handsome. And with that, the edge of her terror dulled, the awful frenzy waned, and second by groping second, her wits fell back in line. When he whispered, "I do know how to reach you, Julie, do I not?" she sighed and let a shudder pass through her body. "Ah, yes, I *want* you to fear me a little. Women should."

With that, his mouth closed swiftly on hers. She felt his bruising lips, and uttered a muffled moan. He laughed and her body recoiled. But his hands still pinned hers to the ground, only his mouth was busy. Her fruitless struggles clearly incited him further. Once his head lifted and he examined her expression with avid eyes. It seemed the most frightening aspect yet, but Julie saw it as her one and only chance. The sob in her throat was real, but her whispered words were designed to win her one brief moment of freedom from his grip.

"The ground is so hard, Duncan. Can't we spread this blanket?"

"Ah, of course," he agreed at once. "No need to be uncomfortable, my darling."

Releasing her hands, he sought to unwind the tangled length of wool from her body without rising. But it resisted his efforts and finally he rose to his knees. Julie, poised, bided her time. It came as he leaned over her, tugging at the stubborn folds. She felt the very moment they loosened, and in that same split second seized and tossed the plaid like a hood over Duncan's head. With her newly freed limbs, she gave a powerful forward thrust. She never waited to see where she had caught him. She was on her feet, running before his breath returned.

In a moment of horror she glimpsed the mare's shadowy outline among the trees *beyond where Duncan struggled to rise*. She dared not try to retrieve Heather. She spun about instead and plunged along the path in the opposite direction, blindly, terrified that her pale sweater would mark her progress ghostlike in the night.

She caught a string of guttural sounds well behind her, and in her mind's eye, she saw Duncan mounting his black. Pursuit was certain, escape impossible. Half-mad with fear, she raced ahead until a bend in the trail provided cover enough that she could dart among the trees unobserved and conceal herself in the dense undergrowth. Half staggering, half falling, she descended a steep incline, landing at last against a huge boulder surrounded by arms of bracken. Panting until she thought her heart must burst, she crawled

around it for refuge. She was afraid to breathe lest her
sobbing gasps be heard. She hugged the ground, straining
to hear, then catching the fast clip-clop clip-clop of
hooves—approaching, coming abreast, hesitating—as
Duncan doubtless wondered where she had gotten to around
that bend. Several times her heart almost stopped, for he
lingered there, before sending the black ahead through the
forest trail in search of what he had nearly achieved.

She had small doubt he would be looking for vengeance,
too. Humiliated, robbed of his dubious pleasure, he was not
the kind to brush it off lightly. He was a man bent on
imposing himself, his physical self and his prowess on
whichever woman defied him. She was quaking with fear
before the last of the hoofbeats faded.

The night had deepened, the moon hidden now behind
seas of clouds roughed by a rising wind. Shivering in her
refuge, Julie wondered how soon she would dare to leave
it to search for Heather. She worried about the little mare
and what they would think at Glenshiel when she did not
return.

After an interminable time she thought of creeping out
and beginning her homeward trek. Surely Duncan would
not search for her through the night. But even as she pon-
dered it, once more she caught the clip-clop of hooves,
distantly this time, and she cowered in her shelter, hugging
the bracken with icy fingers. Then it came to her that the
sound was rising to her from below. It dawned, too, that
at the base of the forest slope, a ribbon of road edged along,
bordering the string of lochen. As if to confirm her discov-
ery, as she peered into the blackness, at a great distance she
caught the twin lights of some nighttime traveler, too far
for the sound of his motor to blot out that other, closer
menace of advancing hoofbeats. Julie held her breath until
the sound neared, came abreast of her hiding place, and
thankfully passed on, fading once again in the distance. She
had no doubt at all it was Duncan, having taken to the road
where he reasoned she might have escaped. When the last
murmur had died, her strength seemed to die with it; surely
he would not return this night. Drained as if a plug had been

pulled, she collapsed on the cold ground and sobbed until every fiber of her body shook with relief. And when that was over, she cried some more, softly now. "Ian, Ian, did it have to be like this?"

CHAPTER FIFTEEN

SHE AWOKE WITH a harsh shriek and a sideways twist of her body. There had been that hot breath on her face and the staggering conviction that he had found her.

"Let me alone!" she screamed. Then she dissolved in tears. "Oh, my God, dear, dear Heather. You've found me."

In a moment she was on her feet, eyes streaming, hugging the gentle creature and rubbing its face with her own. "You wonderful beast, you came looking for me."

It was still too dark to read her own watch. She had no idea how long she had slept. She was stiff from the cold and aching from the hard ground. But she clung to the bay, warming herself against it, until the pounding of her heart slowed.

She felt dirty, and grimy, and limp with weakness. Her legs kept caving in under her. It took all the strength she could muster to climb into the saddle, and then to decide in her confusion which way was home.

Her thinking was still murky, creeping about in clouds of apprehension. For long minutes while Heather stamped the ground impatiently, she slumped with bowed head and listened. Nothing came. What she had thought to be hoof-beats was only the pounding of her heart. Finally it was Heather's sense she turned to. The little bay who had found her in the dark knew the lay of the land far better than she, a newcomer.

She gave it its head, trusting it to take her home.

The journey seemed endless. It had begun to rain, a soft drizzle that drove the cold even deeper into her bones. She was shivering now, and very conscious of the painful swelling of her lips where Duncan had bruised them so savagely. Wiping the water from her face, she flinched over that; and the fiery sting of scratches where the thorny underbrush had raked her forehead and cheeks as she'd dived for cover in her frenzy.

Remembering brought a rush of tears again, and still again. She felt violated, fiercely angry, and sick in turn. She wanted a place to cry it all out until she had cleansed it from her system; yet she knew intuitively no such place existed, and she would never be rid of the horror of this night.

The mare plodded on, and on, until it crossed Julie's mind that Heather, too, might have lost the way. She slumped lower in the saddle, her chin sunk deep into the wet cold wool of her sweater, too dazed any longer to cry. With frozen fingers she extracted a soaked handkerchief from the pocket in her jeans and wiped her dripping nose. Then she sank back disconsolately, blinking the rain from her eyes, peering ahead, then blinking again. Abruptly she straightened in the saddle. Was that—a light? And was the forest thinning here, a little? It was still so dark, it was more like feeling her surroundings rather than seeing them.

But there was no light—or if there was, it had blinked out. No, there it was again. From another angle. Closer by many yards. And brighter. Terror seized her.

Where was she? Where had Heather taken her? Surely not to the lodge again; no, she would have known if they had climbed uphill. But where was this?

Heather snorted and pawed the ground where Julie had brought her to a firm standstill. The light blinked on again, and off. It moved toward her, away, and beyond in a circle, and suddenly as the beam swept past her, Julie knew the forest was at her back. She had come to its fringe. *And the light had found her!*

He'd been waiting. He'd been looking for her all the time she'd slept, knowing she must come this way. Now he was heading for her. Rapidly, but with a queer bobbing, jerking motion. Half fainting, she wheeled Heather about again into the denseness from which they had only emerged. Heather whinnied, *resisting*—of all times, denying Julie's will. For a wild and crazy instant, Julie fought her for control... and then, with a shudder that wracked her body, let the reins go slack, and slumped again, powerless to move, feeling the horse's warm flesh quiver under her; hearing, though dimly now, far back in her senses, a second whinny... a joyful sound, and eager.

With a sob torn from her very heart, she moaned, "Ian, *oh, Ian...*" and woke in his arms on the mossy ground where she had slid from Heather's back.

"Easy, lass, easy," she heard him murmur. "I'll have you in the house in a bit. I can't carry you, Julie, with the crutch. *Over here*, Sandy, this way."

She saw him make a circle with the lantern, and seconds later heard the pound of footsteps. Dazed, she felt herself lifted against a broad, hard chest, her head lolling to one side. She lost consciousness again briefly, but when she drifted back, she lay upon a strange sofa close to a strange hearth where a fire hissed and spat and muttered and flooded her all over with blessed warmth.

Ian was kneeling awkwardly on one leg beside her, but seeing her eyes fluttering open, he called, "It'll be all right, Sandy. Sorry I had to trouble you in the night. Tell Flora I apologize."

"No need," came his mumbled answer. "The lass was

in trouble." When he thudded out the door, she saw Ian rise, and panicked thinking, in her fogged state, that he would go.

"Ian! Don't leave me. I'm so afraid."

He stood gazing down at her, his eyes inscrutable. "You're safe, lass. I'm not going anywhere. This is my croft—my home."

Then it flashed through her darkened mind like a sliver of passing light that it was here Heather had chosen to take her; Ian's croft, no doubt as familiar to her as Glenshiel's stables, and closer perhaps from the point in the forest where the intelligent beast had found her.

Ian's face was as grim as she had ever seen it. After a time, using a single crutch, he hobbled to an adjoining room where Julie could hear water splashing. When he returned, it was with a small basin balanced precariously in his free hand. Awkwardly he knelt again and proceeded to wash the dirt and grime from her face with a soft cloth, working gently around the bruises and painful scratches.

"When I see him again," he muttered, without preamble, "I shall kill him, I swear it."

Her voice trembled. "I don't think you will see him again, Ian. For a while. I—I left my mark. There's blood in the bracken, Ian. Count on it—"

Here a thought swept all else from her mind. She tried to rise, but he urged her gently back. "You're not ready for it, lass."

"But how did you know? Why did you come looking, Ian—"

"Oh, lord, lass, a thousand reasons. Audrey, she came by. She said you'd gone to Duncan at the chalet. I sent her on her way. And fast. I didn't believe her. I—I didn't want to believe that you'd go to him."

"But I did go," Julie began tentatively; the thing needed clearing up. Now in haste, she cleared it, watching its effect on Ian as she recounted Audrey's appalling deception about the accident that never was. "Oh, but that, I'm sure, she did not tell you, Ian, did she?"

She sensed his relief in the way his breath spilled from

his lips. "No. And would you have expected it? The girl tells only what she imagines will benefit her."

He had finished cleaning her face and begun to pat it dry with a rough fresh towel. "Perhaps I have an ointment that will heal the scratches quickly. You look a mess, Mrs. Boland."

"Th-thank you," she said, wearily. "It's words like that that help a girl when she's down." She could not decide whether his lips quirked or not. She felt a lack; as if she expected more. They seemed easy together, and yet he seemed little roused by her presence under his roof.

"You still haven't said why you came looking for me. How did you know I'd come riding from the forest?"

"I didn't. I hoped. I thought, if you stayed with Heather, you'd make it here, or there," he said. "It was Moira telephoned from Glenshiel. You worried them when you didn't return. You—worried us all." And remembering suddenly, "Lord, yes, I'll phone her back now at once."

When he disappeared again into the adjoining room, Julie's eyes moved questioningly among his possessions, many of which, chairs and tables and shelves and cupboards, gave evidence of his own handiwork. The place was indeed small, as Duncan had told her disparagingly, and rough in decor, but the warmth it exuded expanded the space a hundredfold. She sank deeper among the cushions he had surrounded her with, and let escape a small contented sigh. She had not heard him return, crutching his way across his thick sheepskin rugs. She was startled when he spoke from behind her.

"Aye, you are more appealing in that pose than Audrey earlier on."

She sat up, her fatigue falling away. "You mean—"

"That she made a great production of displaying her charms, exactly where you are now."

"And—?"

"And it gained her nothing. And no, I did not lie with her. You should know that."

"And why are you telling me, Ian?" Her voice fluttered badly, asking it.

"Because you are dying to know."

"Why would I care?"

"You care," he said, adding, "and she told me you sent her to me. You told her I was at the croft."

"That's right. You were."

"Were you testing me, Julie?"

"For *what*? She was riding to Glenshiel when we met. I told her you were not there. That you'd gone back to the croft."

"And what made you think I wanted to see her at all?"

She hesitated, then, her voice rising, it came in a little burst from her lips, "Then why have you kept her dangling so long, Ian?" It was a thing that had puzzled and troubled her.

She had come to her feet unsteadily, then moved around to gaze up into his face, a clear challenge in her eyes.

"D-dangling, lass? Are you daft? Have you not heard me on the subject of Audrey Grant?"

"I've heard you speak one thing and act another. If—if you were serious, Ian—" Something was happening to her, a kind of welling in her throat that made it difficult to continue. "If—if you really wanted rid of her—you'd have long ago showed her that stupid note she wrote to Duncan—instead of gloating over it—letting her—letting her wonder and—and guess and keep on hoping. Do you get—some kind of a sadistic pleasure—out of tormenting—"

"*Enough of that, Julie*," he stopped her with a stony look. "You won't tell me how to handle a matter of my own with a woman. And if I thought it right and proper to leave the girl to wonder, and to do a bit of agonizing on her own, I ask you to remember I was hurt. Men have feelings, too, lass. I felt cut to pieces. And I didn't want to talk of it, to her or to anyone, and it was my privilege to handle it the way I liked—*And what on earth are you crying for now, lass?*"

It had finally siezed her, and she buried her face in her hands and gave herself over to that wave of hysteria that had begun in the forest, on the damp earth, when she had cried to him and he was nowhere near. The same that had been gathering and building from the start of their confrontation. Even before, when he had washed the dirt and the blood from her face, and brushed back her hair and stuffed pillows around her for comfort, and built up the fire that she might be warm and dry, and fussed with this and with that . . . and yet, not once, not one little moment had he bent to kiss her! Then they were clashing. Again. As if it must always come to that.

It broke from behind her cupped hands like a cry of pain. "Ian, oh, Ian, *why do we do these things to each other?*"

Off guard, he stared down perplexed and took a step toward her, and another step back. He did not answer, though the moment cried for it. At last, as if his silence were answer enough, her hands slipped from her face that was wet and puckered, and her eyes looked away from his.

"That is all?" she asked, her lips quivering. "When I leave, is that what you will remember? Is it all I can take away with me? That—that our paths once crossed and all we did was b-batter each other, s-senselessly, hurting and hurting and hurting . . . Is that all that's left to take from here?"

He had been inching closer, and now his hand reached and touched her chin, and lifted it until her eyes had no place to look but into his own. His voice fell to her ears a sibilant whisper. "And if you're going, Julie, why would you be wanting to take—anything—with you?"

She was aware he did not ask her to stay. She remembered now, and would remember always that he told her at Glenshiel that he had no wish for her any longer. She had to grope for an answer, one that would say enough, yet not too much. One that would not revive their glib and prickly banter of other days; their very few better moments together, that seemed now in retrospect all light and laughter. She found it finally in the last embers of their dying fire, and she voiced it tremulously, "I would like to know that you will remember me, Ian."

His eyes closed, and he spoke without opening them. "I will never forget you, lass."

Her breath quickened. Then if she was not to see him

again, there was a truth that must be told. For let the day never come when she would reflect on this moment and wish that she had spoken it.

"Then I want you to know, Ian—that I love you."

Having said it, she quailed. Was it too much? Should she have buried it in her heart after all? Why was his face so still, so expressionless? Why had he nothing to say? Even a light-mannered jest would be better than silence.

At last his lips moved, his words almost inaudible. "And why have you been so long saying it, lass?"

She searched his eyes and found them inscrutable. "When did you ask?" she breathed.

"Were my kisses not enough?"

She shook her head. "Kisses are not love, Ian. You must know that now. Love—love is so powerful, Ian, it does not need kisses to survive. When I leave, I know I shall never kiss you again, but," she hesitated, her throat tightening, "but I shall never stop loving you, either."

His hand that had cupped her chin moved suddenly along her cheek, the tips of his fingers losing themselves in her hair. "Then if you love me, Julie, why in the name of common sense are you going away?" And saying it, he bent his head and would have kissed her, but for her hand pressing his lips away.

"I'm listening, Ian," she murmured. "I have not heard it from you yet. Days ago, like a thousand years, it seems, you said you had no wish any longer to hold me. It hurt, Ian. It seared—as if you'd branded the words on my body. I'm listening, Ian, I want to know that wasn't so. I want you to tell me—"

"That I want you? Oh, my God," he breathed. "I love you, Julie. In ways I didn't know I could love. I've loved you, I think, since I first saw you. Even when you infuriated me, I've loved you—and don't ask me why, for I do not know. I've loved and hated you all at once in the same daft moments—it's why we spent so much time arguing—because we weren't making sense."

"Ian." She pressed her hand to his lips again, her eyes

dancing. "Ian, enough! *Now* kiss me. Oh, darling, kiss me now."

"And so you'll not be going after all, my Julie."

They stretched side by side upon the warm sheepskin before the fire. A soft laugh rose from her throat. "Ah, but I will, Ian. You seem to forget."

He reared himself to an elbow, glowering. "Is this a game, lass? Are you playing with me or do we post the banns?"

"*Post the banns*, Ian? Are you mad? I'm still—"

"Oh, lord, forgive me," he growled. "I near forgot. I get so jealous, Julie, when I remember you still belong to another man. I want to ram my fist into the wall!"

"Save your fist, Ian. Your *leg's* still in a splint. And I belong to no one, and never forget it. Only to myself, Ian, which is why I can give myself to whomever I wish."

"*Hold on.*"

"Oh, Ian, stop being so silly. You know whom I wish. Whom I shall always wish."

"It had better be so." Then, after a stretch of silence, "Is that the way you felt when you married Boland?"

Her mind drifted back to that wet November day at home when she had walked down the aisle in the little church above the Sound and met Gary's eyes at the altar. She sighed. "I thought I did. If I hadn't, I wouldn't have married him. Wisdom comes later, Ian, and only with experience. It came late for you, did it not?"

He surprised her, lying back again, chuckling. "I don't know which came first, wisdom or Gran. Gran never cared for Audrey; always saw her the way she was, a climber. Happens she was right, but all I saw for a time was her prettiness. Knew her all my life, but for me she seemed to have bloomed suddenly, after I came home from a couple of years in Australia with my parents. Audrey looked just about right for me then."

"I'm not surprised. She's really gorgeous."

"No longer. Not for me," he said.

"That's a splendid idea," she breathed in his ear.

"Anyway, Gran had a fit when I told her I'd asked Audrey to marry me."

"I cannot imagine your grandmother having a fit," Julie laughed.

"Ay, but that's because Gran's fits are ver-ry subtle. She has them quietly. Stealthily, you might say. That one was so quiet I didn't know how much she'd have given to break the thing up. But, I'll say for the old girl, that's not her way. She told me I was all kinds of a fool, but she went along because I'd already asked Audrey. She doesn't believe in going back on a word. Until the damage was done—of course."

"The damage, you mean when you ran out, and I did you in?"

"She loved you for it, lass. Why do you think she brought you here to Glenshiel?"

"For a thirteenth-century table, I thought."

"Which probably doesn't exist!"

"You're putting me on," Julie gasped, and bolted up beside him.

"Or perhaps it does. I wouldn't know for sure. Lie down, Julie."

She leaned on her elbows studying his face, then traced his lips with a loving finger.

"That'll make trouble for you," he warned.

"Lovely," Julie said. "But are you telling me she saw my marvelous virtues before you did? I once thought she was bent on holding you to your wedding. Honor and all that."

"Honor, eh? Not after I showed her Audrey's letter that first day at the hospital, after Audrey left. Gran was castigating me for bringing shame on the Fraser name. It was the only time I ever saw Gran rattled. She grabbed that letter and wanted immediately to show it around so the whole of Inverness and the north would know why her grandson would not be marrying Audrey Grant. Oh to be sure, most folks thought the accident meant only a delay. Some still do, though some are getting mighty suspicious, circumstances being what they are and nobody talking of a new date.

"For a while I was tempted to go along with Gran, advertising the little witch for what she was. It was hurting a lot. But och, Julie, I knew what would come of it. Audrey would be shamed right out of the glen. She'd never have a chance at another lad; never live it down."

"But what of you, Ian? Will you ever live it down?"

After a thoughtful moment he answered quietly, "You know it is easier on a man than on a woman. Shouldn't be, but it is. In time it'll all fade away. The important thing is, *I* know I did right. I forgave her her romp in the dell with Duncan; there was no reason I had to forgive her the rest. Gran and I talked, and we finally pledged each other we'd never discuss it. I'd never even have told you, Julie, except for all the scorn you were heaping on me. I didn't like that. I didn't want you remembering that against me when you'd gone."

A small sigh fell from her lips. "It is not what I would have remembered, Ian, if I'd gone."

He smiled, and tightened his arm around her. "As for Audrey, I don't care if she finds another lad and soon. I hope she does. The whole thing will simmer down and be forgotten then."

"I hope that for her, too, Ian," Julie agreed. "I had the impression from talking to her that she's insecure enough as it is. Her background bothers her. She was almost defiant telling me how her people had come up from the docks at Aberdeen. As if that were some kind of a crime to be lived down."

"Aye, she made too much of that," he responded. "Besides, that was two generations ago. And I don't know why she would want to live it down anyway. But then, she never took enthusiastically to my croft, either, or me working on it. No wonder the thought of being a Lady was more than she could resist." He paused, then with a grim laugh, added, "It must have been a terrible moment for her waiting to see if Duncan would show up to claim her before the wedding."

"Oh, yes, Ian. I remember how nervous she seemed. I was that close up I could see her when she arrived. And—" she laughed, "I thought she was frightened of her wedding night."

"Och, not her," he said. "Not after the dell, anyway. Forget her, lass, come kiss me. And what is wrong now? Why that unhappy look on your face?"

"That letter, Ian," she said with a new firmness. "You know Audrey'll come around, still wanting you, if she never knows you've got it. And I might just possibly get into a terrible battle with her."

"Aye, that would be worth seeing."

"I am serious, Ian. You'll never be rid of her if you don't hand it back. And stop laughing, please. It's not a bit funny. I think you're getting a fiendish delight out of keeping her in the dark about it, aren't you?"

"Julie, Julie," he said, his long arms reaching for her. "I had my fiendish delight with her, earlier, lass. Before you arrived. When she stretched out on my sofa, and I went and got the letter from a drawer, and showed it to her, and tore it into wee bits and stuffed them down her blouse, and saw her fly out of the door and gallop off, and all the time not a word did I speak to her! And you'll not be troubled by her again, I promise you. And if you can stop laughing long enough, won't you kiss me now so I can get on with making up your bed for the night? It is late, and tomorrow will be a busy one."

"Oh, I forgot," she mumbled, her mouth still clinging to his. "Your grandmother returns tomorrow."

"Aye, Moira has told me. The fun begins." He started rising clumsily, but she restrained him.

"Ian, what's wrong with—right here, for tonight?"

He lay back again, peering at her through half-shut eyes. "Both of us?" And with a grin, "You trust me?"

"No. And neither do I trust myself." She laughed. "It will be an exercise in discipline, and good practice considering that there'll be a bit of a wait for my divorce."

"How long, for heaven's sake?" He wailed it, and she

saw he had not thought of it until this moment.

"About half a year to go," she murmured in his ear. "Oh, don't look so horrified. It could have been longer if I hadn't been so clever and started proceedings half a year back."

He was up on his elbow again. "Julie, *a whole half of a year?*"

She swallowed, the reality of it beginning to confront her. "That's right," she said softly.

"And what if the bloke says no? What if they can't even find him?"

She went thoughtful, coping again with the raging anger that had seized her following her talk with Shirley on the phone.

"They will find him," she said at last. "And I guarantee," she added, "the bloke will not say no. Let's sleep, love."

"Who can sleep?" he muttered. "Six months?"

She giggled. "Or perhaps when your leg is out of the splint, finally, whichever comes first. Unless you've smashed your fist by then!"

"Snuggle close and be silent, lass, before you talk us into it."

CHAPTER SIXTEEN

"AND CAN YOU be happy here, Julie?"

They stood together on the bluff overlooking that necklace of lochen that so few days before she had viewed from the opposite slope with Duncan.

The day was Scotland's day; chill with wind and sudden showers, and great puffballs of clouds vaulting over the glen. While all about them life moved on as it had in this rugged land since time immemorial. At their backs Ian's croft snugged low upon the ground where it had sat for centuries.

"It was a crumbled ruin when I came to it," he explained. "There was nothing but the fireplace stone, and part of the outer walls. I rebuilt it, and added to it and I want you very much to be happy in it, lass. Since it is unlikely I can ever make you rich."

She could barely restrain the tears. "How can I not be happy if you're there, Ian?"

"It's what I hoped, Julie."

He turned to shout to one of his men emerging from the byre. It was the same who had carried her indoors in the night. "Sandy, I thank you kindly for your help, and I hope Flora was not distressed."

"Och no, Ian. Flora says she'll come and do for the lady if there's need."

They had moved together, and Julie smiled and offered her hand. "I thank you, too, Sandy. I'm Julie Boland——"

"Soon to be Julie Fraser," Ian announced to the other's delight.

"Oooh, and is it so?" Sandy exclaimed. "Flora will be delighted, and all the gir-rls. My daughters. I have four. Ye must come to tea, then, with us soon. We're just over the brae, aye, that one before ye."

Julie was too moved for words, but especially over Ian's warm relationship with his workers. "I like that," she told him when they were alone. "I like the way you get along with your people. There are others?"

"A lad or two. And Sandy's young daughters who come by to do my washing and ironing and little tasks they do better than I to earn a pound or two."

Julie giggled. "I'm sure Audrey noticed *that*."

"Oo, aye, those were the 'women' she accused me of having on the side. And will you?"

"I shall keep you too busy to notice anything female around here, Ian, I promise."

"Except for the ewes at lambing time," he laughed.

"I shall help you," she said, eagerly all at once. "Oh, Ian, there's so much to learn after——after I come back."

"Damn it, Julie, I hate your going. I'll miss you and worry the bloke won't let you go."

Her laugh was cynical. "He will, Ian. Have no doubt. I didn't tell you, but he is back at my house. My friend, Shirley Wickam told me when I phoned her."

"*He's back*? Looking for you? Then I'm going with you."

She smiled. "It won't be necessary. I can handle him," she answered serenely. "I know what he wants."

"He wants *you*. Why else did he come back. He loves you."

"He *needs* me, Ian. *His* words. To him it's one and the same. I made life easy for him. He didn't have to think. He didn't have to go out and face that mean old competitive world. He had a big, comfortable house to live in, and meals like his mother never cooked. The only reason he walked away from it at all was because he never doubted it would be there when he got back."

"But he'll fight the divorce now. He's not going to see it all go down the drain."

She shook her head, almost sadly. "Gary is no fighter. It takes effort to fight, and some ingenuity. Besides, when push comes to shove, Ian, I am, above all, his pocketful of cash. After I've dissolved my partnership with Shirley, which I shall do, and when I've disposed of my property, Gary will have a choice of fighting, or accepting a nice, flat, one-time sum. Knowing him, I'll guarantee he'll take the money and run. Oh, there'll be all sorts of sentimental claptrap about not being able to live without me—which he has just disproven by rambling around the country happily enough alone, and never a suggestion that I join him. I am unimpressed any longer by Gary Boland's everlasting *need*. For I have needs of my own—" the last with a sly smile, and a sudden whisper, "that are going to keep you very, very busy when I get back, Ian."

"How soon, for heaven's sake?" he asked, folding her in his arms.

"About a month? Perhaps? As soon as I've started things rolling. Maybe less. How does that sound?"

"Like I'm not going to be worth a damn for a month, lass. But then, when you're back, do you know what'll happen? Gran will commandeer you and keep you at Glenshiel to make sure all is quite proper. And she will find at least half a dozen reasons each week to spend the night at her suite in Inverness and she will be very certain to announce it to you in advance. And to make her car available to you, or Heather if you prefer."

"Oh, darling," she laughed, hugging him. "Come on, we must go see her. She's due in the hour."

"When I've kissed you, lass," he said. She glanced about, seeing Sandy and a young helper urging sheep up a ramp into a lorry for transport to the winter pastures.

"Here? Now?"

"For all the world to witness, Julie. Look, world!" he shouted. "I am going to kiss my bride!"

The day had come.

She had gone to sleep at Glenshiel—her third night since Mairi Mackay's return—dreading it. In the morning she knew Ian would arrive for breakfast, which would be unduly quiet except for Mairi's chirping non sequiturs; Mairi, happy as a lark on learning their news, kept tossing them about like rose petals as if she had run out of causes to embrace, now that she had returned from the home of her eighty-two-year-old brother whose very existence, like the table, Julie had begun to doubt. Especially so, after Mairi confided the curious observation that, "I had a feeling when I left something like this might happen."

Julie had taken a moment to study her. "You didn't— plan it this way, Mairi?" she queried.

"Good heavens, no, my dear. I never intervene. I merely set the stage, as it were, and let the actors play their roles. It rarely fails. Once I managed to bring Ian to Glenshiel, he played Ian to the life! And you, my dear, were a charming and, I thought, predictable Julie. As for Audrey, poor lass, she played Audrey to the hilt; my only problem there being trying to keep them apart."

"But why, Mairi, knowing how Ian felt about her finally?"

"That was *exactly* why, Julie. I did not want her to leave here some day with her pretty face—ah, rearranged, as it were."

Her smile was Ian's, Julie thought, with the same teasing quirk.

"But no," she added, "I did not approve of his withholding that letter from Audrey herself. And he knew it, and we clashed about that a bit, Ian insisting I was invading his affairs too much, and yowling about wanting to go to his croft—but only at first. After that, it was nothing but acting, and very poor acting, I decided. You will agree." Mairilike, that last was a statement, Julie thought, not a query.

At breakfast on this last day, Julie's eyes kept clinging to Ian's, and beneath the linen cloth their hands linked again and again. She could almost not bear to think ahead, when she must tell him good-bye at the station. Everything that had happened since she arrived now seemed so unreal. She kept fighting off a conviction that as the train carried her south, and down, down from the Highlands, it would all disappear, as if it had never been. And that when she came back looking for him, people would say, "Who? Och no, there is no such mon aboot here. Nor ever was . . ."

"Oh, my dear," Mairi broke in once, "about the table—"

Julie looked across at her blankly, then uttered a small cry, "Yes, the table," knowing she had completely forgotten it.

"I cannot imagine where it is stored," Mairi said. "Alec tells me he has looked through all the crates and odd pieces."

"*Gran.*" Ian addressed her with lowered head, eyeing her reproachfully under his brows.

"Yes, Ian?"

He laughed. "You know very well, Gran."

For a few seconds their twin smiles dueled. Then Mairi inquired, "My dear boy, are you questioning my integrity?"

"Not at all, Gran, never would I question that. It is the thirteenth-century table I question. Now tell us, old girl, was there ever such a one?"

Mairi, tall in her chair, skewered him with a frigid look. "Now won't you feel like a complete fool, my dear boy," she said, "when it turns up—as your wedding gift?"

"Mairi! Oh, oh, we thank you so much. Ian, isn't that lovely?"

"Aye, Gran. Forgive my big mouth."

"Never," said Mairi Mackay. "And it is time you two got started, if Julie is to catch her train."

The day was unseasonably mild, almost warm for that time of the year, as Ian took the wheel of the old Jag, his splinted left leg settled gingerly between them. Soon they left Glenshiel behind, rolling past hillocks lying gold green in the sun, past rock-strewn braes and sparkling burns racing to the lochs, past clumps of grazing sheep, their shorn coats renewing for the winter; past all those many scenes that in so short a time Julie had grown to love.

"That's St. Ninian's," she said, suddenly sitting erect.

"It is, lass. It'll be there for us when you return."

He reached over and squeezed her hand and she giggled, "What if you don't show up—again, Ian?"

"Send my head off to be examined. Oh, Julie, I love you so." His voice underwent a change, reflecting anxiety. "I'm far more worried it's you who'll change your mind. It's a mistake," he added earnestly, "to let you go off alone. I feel it."

"Oh come on, Ian, how else can it be done?"

"What if the sight of him brings things back—"

"Oh, Ian, what if unicorns dance on the moon!"

He went silent. Moments later he mumbled, "I still think it's a stupid mistake." But she did not answer. She was studying the route they drove that seemed familiar to her all at once.

Abruptly her heart quickened. She knew where she was. This was the road she had driven just before intruding on the wedding party all those weeks before. And up ahead, there it was, the cut in the braes that was the steep incline of that other road she had taken in error. The laughter spilling from her throat brought a frown from Ian.

"Slow down, darling," she breathed. "Listen—*what if?*" Her eyes teased mercilessly. "What if we turned onto that road ahead?"

"Across the Beauly braes?" he asked, bewildered.

"That one," she nodded. "Oh, do take it, Ian, please."

"You'll miss your train," he pointed out hopefully.

"Good. There's a later one."

"All ri-ight," he said. Turning sharply left, the Jag took the winding climb to the top with only minor wheezes and groans.

"Now," she said when they could look down from the upper world into the glen, "'what if' I told you—"

"You're rubbing it in, lass. What's on your mind?"

"Drive, darling, and when you get to the road to Abriachan, stop for a moment so I can tell you about 'mistakes' and their dire consequences."

"You're making sport of me."

"Because I love you," she laughed, blowing a kiss his way.

He grinned, relaxed once more, and pressed on at a lazy crawl until the junction came into view.

"There, stop there," Julie said, her eyes glowing. When he did, she stepped to the ground where the two roads met.

"There," she called to him. "I just had to touch down at the place where a 'stupid mistake' turned my life around. Oh, darling, do you know how close I came to never knowing you at all? *This close.* If I'd turned to the right here, I'd have found the shops I came looking for in Beauly, and perhaps pulled off some fabulous deal. But I took the left turn by mistake, Ian, and—I found *you.*"

She was back beside him in the car, leaning to him, his eyes bathing her in warmth.

"That was no mistake, lass," he murmured. "That was Someone Up There giving you a little shove, telling you, 'There's a handsome laddie waiting for you this way, and a lot of dead bric-a-brac that way. Now which do you choose?' And of course you chose the wrong way which was the right way."

"Stop it, Ian," she laughed, burying her face on his shoulder. "It was *fate*—or, no it wasn't that, either. It was—" She broke off, her thoughts abruptly in turmoil. A long silence after, she said, "Darling, would you drive the Abriachan road into town?"

"Gladly," he agreed. "It'll take a little longer."

"Yes, I know."

"Any special reason?" he asked, turning into the narrow

track she had traveled before.

She hesitated. A thought had seized her that was so preposterous, she could not even speak of it to Ian. For all he spoke of Someone Up There, he'd think she was mad if she said aloud, there's Someone I knew who walked these lands a hundred years ago. And if anyone could have arranged what happened to us, from her vantage point Up There, it has be to Ishbel MacDonald. Now I want to pass her way and tell her, Thanks, Gran, thank you kindly.

But of course she could not tell Ian that. All he had to know was, "I like it here."

"Aye," he said. "No more tranquil a place in the world. When you're over there getting your affairs in order, lass, I'll come by here now and then and remember how radiant you're looking now. And how I want to take you in the heather this minute."

Her laughter was soft, soft as a trickling burn. When he pulled to the side of the road and stopped, she went into his arms. "I love you, Ian," she whispered. And, "There *is* a *very* late train," she said.

Second Chance at Love ™

WINDS OF MORNING #13
by Laurie Marath
Lovely Jennifer Logan believed she'd left troubled love far behind when she came to Glengarriff, the small village on Ireland's coast...until she met the most difficult, haunted—and completely wonderful—man in the world!

HARD TO HANDLE #14
by Susanna Collins
The Belgian aristocrat is a supremely talented equestrian and trainer, an arrestingly handsome, passionate man. But the moment beautiful, widowed Ariane Charles sees him, she knows he's more dangerous to her than an untamed stallion.

BELOVED PIRATE #15
by Margie Michaels
The crystal waters of the Bahamas hold the treasure-find of a lifetime...and the test of a lifetime, too, for stunning Lorelei Averill as she meets again the man she'd once loved too well.

PASSION'S FLIGHT #16
by Marilyn Mathieu
Cool and elusive as a spring mist, Beverly Milford resists the devastating charm of the celebrated lover who is her boss. In Paris, then Hawaii, her defenses erode and the lovely widow is in emotional peril...again.

HEART OF THE GLEN #17
by Lily Bradford
Roaming the byways of Scotland, scouting for antiques, Julie Boland encounters sharp-tongued Ian Fraser. His attractions are enormous, his emotions seem as fickle as her faithless ex-husband's... can the handsome laird erase Julie's bitter memories?

BIRD OF PARADISE #18
by Winter Ames
Brilliant as she is beautiful, Sara Mancini continues her agricultural experiments on Eric Thoreson's Panamanian coffee plantation—despite the interference of her late husband's family...of the tempestuous Rima...and of her irresistible employer.

**TO GET THESE BREATHLESS TALES
OF LOVERS LOST AND FOUND
PLEASE USE THE ORDER FORM
ON THE FOLLOWING PAGE**

Second Chance at Love ™

Jove's Thrilling New Romance Line